Bestsellers
Can Be
Murder

Connie Shelton

Books by Connie Shelton

THE CHARLIE PARKER MYSTERY SERIES

Deadly Gamble
Vacations Can Be Murder
Partnerships Can Be Murder
Small Towns Can Be Murder
Memories Can Be Murder
Honeymoons Can Be Murder
Reunions Can Be Murder
Competition Can Be Murder
Balloons Can Be Murder
Obsessions Can Be Murder
Gossip Can Be Murder
Stardom Can Be Murder
Phantoms Can Be Murder
Buried Secrets Can Be Murder
Legends Can Be Murder
Weddings Can Be Murder
Alibis Can Be Murder
Escapes Can Be Murder
Sweethearts Can Be Murder
Money Can Be Murder
Road Trips Can Be Murder
Cruises Can Be Murder
Deceptions Can Be Murder
Bestsellers Can Be Murder
Old Bones Can Be Murder - a Halloween novella
Holidays Can Be Murder - a Christmas novella

THE SAMANTHA SWEET COZY MYSTERY SERIES

Sweet Masterpiece
Sweet's Sweets
Sweet Holidays
Sweet Hearts
Bitter Sweet
Sweets Galore
Sweets Begorra
Sweet Payback
Sweet Someethings
Sweets Forgotten
Spooky Sweet
Sticky Sweet
Sweet Magic
Deadly Sweet Dreams
The Ghost of Christmas Sweet
Tricky Sweet
Haunted Sweets
Secret Sweets
Garden Sweets
Spellbound Sweets - a Halloween novella
Thankful Sweets - a Thanksgiving novella
The Woodcarver's Secret

THE HEIST LADIES SERIES

Diamonds Aren't Forever
The Trophy Wife Exchange
Movie Mogul Mama
Homeless in Heaven
Show Me the Money

THE BEN PECOS MYSTERY SERIES

The Homecoming

Bestsellers Can Be Murder

Charlie Parker Mysteries, Book 24

Connie Shelton

Secret Staircase Books

Bestsellers Can Be Murder
Published by Secret Staircase Books, an imprint of
Columbine Publishing Group, LLC
PO Box 416, Angel Fire, NM 87710

Copyright © 2026 Connie Shelton
All rights reserved. No part of this book may be reproduced or transmitted in any form or by any means, electronic or mechanical, including photocopying, recording, or by an information storage and retrieval system without permission in writing from the publisher. No portion of this book may be used for the training of any artificial intelligence (AI) model without express written permission from the publisher and compensation paid to the author.
This book is a work of fiction. Names, characters, places and incidents are either the product of the author's imagination or are used fictitiously. Any resemblance to actual events or locales or persons, living or dead, is entirely coincidental. Although the author and publisher have made every effort to ensure the accuracy and completeness of information contained in this book we assume no responsibility for errors, inaccuracies, omissions, or any inconsistency herein. Any slights of people, places or organizations are unintentional.

Book layout and design by Secret Staircase Books
Cover images © Igor Zakharevich, Elias Bitar
First trade paperback edition: March, 2026
First e-book edition: March, 2026

* * *

Publisher's Cataloging-in-Publication Data

Shelton, Connie
Bestsellers Can Be Murder / by Connie Shelton.
p. cm.
ISBN 978-1649142375 (paperback)
ISBN 978-1649142382 (e-book)

1. Charlie Parker (Fictitious character)—Fiction. 2. Australia—Fiction. 3. Private Investigators—Fiction. 4. Women sleuths—Fiction. I. Title

Charlie Parker Mystery Series : Book 24.
Shelton, Connie, Charlie Parker mysteries.

BISAC : FICTION / Mystery & Detective.
813/.54

For all of my readers... thank you so much!

Chapter 1

People say you can often know, somehow, when the phone is about to ring. Some actually claim to know when the call will be a momentous one. On this weekday morning, I must confess that I didn't have a clue.

At 7:42 a.m., Albuquerque was already sunstruck—every street bathed in light, our quiet little business neighborhood dusted with early-morning calm. The windows in my office reflected the green of late-summer trees and a cloudless blue sky.

With Ron out of the office all week, I'd achieved something close to the mythic 'zero inbox,' or at least the paper equivalent: every manila folder filed, every sticky note either dealt with or transferred to the appropriate case log, my laptop screen split between an open spreadsheet and the digital address book for RJP Investigations. It was the rarest sort of day, one that felt entirely my own, as if the universe had granted me a brief and precious reprieve from human chaos. Our little brown and white spaniel sprawled contentedly on the rug beside my desk, a testament to the calm.

I took a victory sip from my coffee—black this time, though Drake was often lobbying to get me on board with his latest flavored creamer obsession—and scrolled through my tasks for the day, each one color-coded by priority and actual client deadline. Nothing on fire. No urgent client calls, no crisis emails from my brother and business partner, Ron. The only sound was the faint whir of the A/C from the building's aging ductwork. For one short moment, I toyed with the idea of getting ahead on next week's billing, but ducking out early so Freckles and I could take a walk in the Bosque, before the August heat morphed into one of our seasonal monsoon rains sounded like more fun.

So, when my cell phone erupted with the opening bars of "Winchester Cathedral"—which I recognized as the ringtone I'd assigned to my Aunt Louisa—I nearly spilled coffee on my clean desktop.

I wiped a stray drop from my desk calendar and thumbed the answer button. "Louisa! To what do I owe the pleasure?"

I heard a brief, clattering noise—a background of plates or cups colliding in the echoing way only British kitchens have—followed by her voice, enthusiastic as a college radio DJ, which spilled through the line.

"Charlie, darling! I've had the most spectacular idea, and I need you to say yes before you come up with one of your many, many reasons why you can't."

I stifled a chuckle. "Can we define 'spectacular' first? Is this one of those ideas that requires tequila shots, or will a pot of strong tea do it?"

"Neither, both, it doesn't matter!" she said, her voice leaping an octave. "I've found the perfect flight and a darling little boutique hotel in Sydney—Sydney, Australia, not the one in Canada—and I want us to go together. It'll be a proper bucket list adventure. Two weeks, the two of us. I'm picturing us by the harbor, with the Opera House in the background and you trying to teach me how to use a selfie stick without impaling a stranger."

I pinched the bridge of my nose and let silence speak for a few seconds. Louisa, true to form, interpreted it as an opening.

"I know you're swamped with work and that you're the brilliantly responsible one," she added, "but honestly, Charlie, I haven't been out of the UK in over a year, and you—you admitted recently you needed a break. Or has the American work ethic finally finished what the IRS started and ground you into a fine, caffeinated powder?"

"Some of us," I said, tracing swirls on the desk with a fingertip, "are small business owners who can't drop everything on an impulse. Even if it's a bucket-list whim."

"Nonsense," she replied. "You've told me on several occasions that your brother's perfectly capable of running the place while you're away. And you do owe me, remember?"

I heard a clink—a teaspoon striking china, I guessed. The memory of her tiny Bury St. Edmunds home came into focus, all artfully mismatched mugs and the sweet, yeasty aroma of home-baked bread.

"I seem to recall," Louisa went on, "that you were the one who swore, and I quote, 'Someday we'll travel the world together, like Thelma and Louise, only with less crime and better snacks.' Well, I'm ready for less crime and better snacks, darling."

She had a way of making every conversation feel like a dare.

"Out of curiosity," I said, "how much research did you do before calling me at—" I checked my computer screen—"before eight o'clock in the morning, local time?"

"Darling, it's mid-afternoon here," she said, feigning offense. "I spent the entire day on TripAdvisor getting ideas and asked the man at the travel agency if he could find us seats next to each other. You should have heard his reaction when I told him we're doing a great-aunt-niece adventure. They adore me in that office, you know."

I believed it. Louisa's charisma was the sort that left people slightly dazed, like they'd accidentally signed up for a college course, but a really charming one where the only rule was mandatory fun.

I rolled my chair away from the desk and looked out the window. The Sandias were blue at the edges, the day sharpening. I tried to imagine myself halfway around the world—Sydney, of all places, with the ocean as backdrop and the southern hemisphere sky looking completely unfamiliar—and my brain stuttered. The thought was so out of sequence with my day-to-day that I almost laughed.

"We have clients," I said, the words sounding less forceful than I intended. "Some of them actually pay us on time if we deliver answers for them. We've got three active investigations. And I can't simply drop off the face of the planet for two weeks."

"You can if the other half of your investigative firm is named Ron Parker. Your brother knows how to handle anything short of a full-blown international incident," Louisa countered, not missing a beat. "Besides, I've spoken to Drake, and he's promised to keep your plants alive and your dog happy while you're gone."

I turned from the window, trying not to smile. "You called my husband before you called me?"

"He's more easily persuaded than you are, honestly, and he's so impossibly nice."

That much was true. I let out a sigh that was half resignation, half amusement. "I'll have to check and see if my passport's expired."

"You renewed it last year. I remember."

She was right. I swiveled back to my perfectly clear desk. This was surely the sign that it was fine for me to leave for two weeks. And Louisa was correct—Ron could handle whatever came through the door in my absence.

Louisa was talking again, describing the walking tours she'd mapped out and the food markets she wanted to try. "You haven't lived," she said, "until you've had a lamington, straight from the source. And I want us to go on a ferry ride. Or at least eat ice cream while watching the ferries. Are you writing this down?"

"I'm still processing the part where you want me to fly halfway around the planet with zero notice," I said, but as I did, I opened a browser tab and typed 'Albuquerque to Sydney flight time.'

She must have heard the change in my tone, because her voice softened a notch. "Charlie, I know you. If you put this off, you'll find a dozen reasons not to go, and one day you'll wake up and wonder why you waited. The world is full of reports to file and clients to bill, but opportunities to make memories? Those are a little harder to come by."

It was such a Louisa thing to say—sentimental without being cloying, a direct hit to the guilt center of my brain. I watched the search results populate on my laptop: 18 hours, minimum, plus the lost day to the International Date Line. It was insane. And also exactly the sort of thing I used to promise myself I'd do once I'd grown into an adult who didn't need to double-check the balance of her checking account before committing to a trip.

A small voice in my head—a quieter, braver version of myself—whispered that maybe the time was now.

"All right," I said. "If I can find flights for under four grand, and if Ron doesn't throw a fit, and if you promise not to drag me to any haunted penal colonies, I'll consider it."

Louisa's squeal was so loud I jerked the phone away from my ear.

"I've got the airfares covered. I'll phone my travel agent this minute and have him finalize everything for both of us," she said. "This will be epic. I'll send your itinerary as soon as we hang up, and as you're packing don't forget it's the tail-end of winter there. Could be rainy."

"Got it." I'd clicked over to the weather app to check out the forecast.

"And Charlie? Thank you. I mean it. You're my favorite niece—my only one—but it counts."

I'd always admired her ability to seize joy wherever it appeared—because I'd never been quite as good at it myself. I was probably too much like my scientist father, whereas his only sister was completely into *carpe diem*.

"Send the email," I said. "I'm excited to see the details."

We said our goodbyes—Louisa's full of exclamation points. I set the phone on my desk; it proceeded to buzz with incoming texts and links to TripAdvisor reviews.

When I opened Louisa's email, it was three screens long, complete with emojis, attachments, and a detailed list of possible activities broken down by day. At the very end, she'd pasted a quote in bold, purple font: "Life shrinks or expands in proportion to one's courage." —Anaïs Nin.

Well, no one was going to call me chicken. I closed my laptop and leaned back in my chair, imagining the world down under, waiting for me like a dare I couldn't resist.

Before I could talk myself out of it, I shot a quick text off to Ron: **I'm taking two weeks off to see Louisa. Any problem?**

A puzzled-looking emoji appeared, along with the words: **I guess not.**

My message to Drake was done in a teasing tone (I called him sneaky-pants for talking to Louisa about the trip before I knew of it). He responded with a string of hearts, telling me to relax and have fun.

So, okay … down inside I knew I was really doing this.

* * *

It must have been nearly midnight in England when Louisa phoned the second time, having bombarded my email with links, pages of flight information, and separate messages for every fun activity she could think of. I'd skimmed it all, hoping we could wait until we were together to decide on how we would spend our time.

"Did you see the glamping link?" Louisa said, not bothering to greet me. "I could spend a week floating in those infinity pools. Oh, and the hotel concierge says they organize sunrise yoga on the rooftop. You should see the view. Wait, I'm forwarding you another email. Are you sitting down?"

"I'm at work," I said, "which is functionally the same as sitting down."

Louisa ignored this. "I've booked our arrival for the fourteenth. That gives you two weeks to prepare. And before you start worrying about the cost, I have enough frequent flyer points to cover all of it. So, the only thing standing in our way is your pathological fear of spontaneity."

I could almost hear her grinning through the phone, the words tumbling over one another in their rush to the finish line.

Her tone softened, "I know it's a big ask. You have your work, and your life, and a husband who's probably going to spoil that dog rotten while you're away. But Charlie, I really want this."

I smiled. "You really don't need to pay for everything."

"I'll throw in travel insurance," she said, ignoring my protest, "and you know how much I loathe insurance companies. Plus, you don't really have to take time off. Bring your laptop and consider it remote fieldwork. Investigate the Australian psyche. Research the underbelly of the international breakfast buffet. The opportunities for observation are limitless."

I snorted. "I think you want a travel partner to keep you from being attacked by poisonous spiders."

"That's a bonus," she replied, deadpan. "But seriously. This could be my last big trip, you know. The knees aren't getting any younger, and the doctor says I'm supposed to avoid 'strenuous travel,' which I've chosen to interpret as not running for trains, rather than skipping the trips altogether."

There it was. The gentle, inevitable tug of mortality. Louisa's secret weapon.

"All right. If you've really got the points and the hotel, it looks like we're doing it."

The scream that followed was loud enough to get Freckles' attention, and she raised her head from across the office to stare at me.

"Best niece ever! Oh, you won't regret it. I'll send you the finalized flight details, the hotel links, and a map of the city. And a packing list. Should I book any day trips? We could see the Blue Mountains. Or learn to surf. Or drink wine at the harbor for a week." Louisa laughed. "Never mind. We'll decide all that later."

"Spontaneity will be our watchword."

She laughed, delighted. "It's a deal. Oh, Charlie, this is going to be wonderful. I've already started packing. Basically, the essentials—books, sunscreen, a hat for every occasion."

I thought of my own packing style—minimal, efficient, thinking about what could be left behind rather than what to bring. Maybe this time, I'd try it her way.

"See you in Sydney," I said, and meant it.

Chapter 2

I've watched enough episodes of *Border Security* to be fairly anxious about the questions I would face at Sydney International. The customs folks were notorious for pinning people down on what contraband items they might be carrying, and on the TV show some were detained for hours.

But, apparently, I didn't fit the profile of a master drug smuggler. Everyone I spoke to was friendly. I retrieved my bag, and when I answered the questions about medications I might have with me (luckily, none), I was passed directly through.

The arrivals area seemed filled with a million moving bodies, conversations in a dozen languages floating through the air. Families clustered around the ropes, holding up signs and flowers and helium balloons in every possible shade of "Welcome Home." I scanned for Louisa, expecting the familiar petite, gray-haired woman in British clothing, holding a printed sign or a paper flower, something discreet.

Instead, I spotted her from fifty yards away, a comet in the sea of greeters. She wore a caftan of vivid purple with a strand of turquoise beads and—because it was Louisa—an enormous sunhat meant for a day at Bondi Beach rather than a dim air terminal. Her arrival two days earlier had clearly given her time to acclimate.

She caught my gaze and lit up like a Christmas tree, waving both arms overhead as if signaling a ship in distress. A few heads turned. I considered ducking behind the nearest pillar, but too late.

"Charlie!" she shrieked, weaving through the barricades with the deftness of a seasoned air traveler.

I barely had time to unshoulder my computer case before she enveloped me in a hug. Her perfume was exactly as I remembered: floral, but with an undertone of black pepper that lingered. She pulled back, inspecting my face with both hands.

"I can't believe you're here," she said, as if I'd arrived by magic rather than a commercial flight she'd arranged herself. "You must be shattered. Are you shattered? I warned you about the time difference, but you probably worked up until the minute you left, didn't you?"

"It was only a ten-hour day," I said, with a twist to my grin. "And I did manage to sleep on the final leg of the flight out of Honolulu."

She patted my cheek. "You poor thing. But look at you! You look *wonderful*, darling."

I spotted a money exchange booth and nodded toward it. "I'll need some cash."

She laughed, a noise so bright and sharp it made my head ring. "Whatever for? Everything here is done with a tap of a card. You're here. That's what counts. And I have so much to show you, you have no idea. I found a thermal pool in the city, and they say it's the thing to do for jet lag. Oh, and I've reserved a harbor cruise. A small one, but the views—"

"Louisa," I said, raising a hand. "Can we start with offloading my bags at the hotel and getting a cup of tea?"

"Are you hungry? I've discovered amazing pastries here."

I shook my head. They feed you well in business class, another happy surprise when I realized what a splurge my aunt had done for me.

She grinned, looping her arm through mine and steering me toward the exit. It occurred to me, as we walked, that I had never seen Louisa look healthier or more animated in my life. The last few years, her emails and phone calls had been laced with references to 'the knees' and 'the hip' and 'the arthritis,' but here she moved with a spring that belonged to a much younger woman.

"You look good," I said, and meant it.

She squeezed my arm. "Sydney suits me. Or quite possibly it's the thought of two weeks with you, my dear. Tell me all about the flight. Were there any screaming babies? Did you get the aisle seat like I asked?"

I recounted, in as few words as possible, the litany of minor in-flight indignities: the woman across the aisle who'd coughed the entire way from LAX to Honolulu, the lavatory with water splashes all over the teensy vanity top, the man in 3B who had refused to wear shoes at any time. Louisa ate up every detail, nodding as if mentally cataloging the information for later use.

The airport doors hissed open, and the outside air wrapped around us—a chilly, salty humidity under an overcast sky I hadn't expected in August. I could smell the ocean here at the edge of the city. Louisa took a deep breath, smiling as if she'd orchestrated the weather herself.

"Here's the plan," she said, eyes sparkling. "We take the train straight to Circular Quay, drop your bags at the hotel, and get a proper breakfast. After that, we'll walk the harbor and see if the rumors about the world's best flat white are true. I've mapped out every possible walking tour, but don't worry, I'll go easy on you until you're fully acclimated. Oh! Did I tell you about Sydney Park? Or the book signing?"

"You didn't," I said, but she was fishing two plastic cards from her bottomless purse, hands moving with the precision of a street magician.

I took my Opal Card—apparently the way to get about in Sydney—and followed, my mind lagging two or three sentences behind her at all times. The world outside the airport blurred by: palm trees, glass towers, a distant curve of water. The train platform was packed with a medley of travelers and locals—schoolchildren in uniforms, business types checking phones, a pair of backpackers debating the ethics of eating kangaroo.

Louisa found us seats and plopped down, fanning herself with a brochure she'd nabbed from the tourism rack. "Do you want to know something funny?" she said, leaning in close. "I've dreamed about this trip for years. Not only Sydney, but this exact train ride. The first time I was here—God, it must've been 1978—I was so broke I had to walk from the airport into the city. Took four hours.

I vowed I'd return someday, with enough money to ride the train and stay somewhere with actual towels."

She grinned. "And now I get to share it with you. Life's a miracle, isn't it?"

I watched the city unfold through the train's glistening windows, the skyline growing closer, sharper, more real.

"You know," I said, as we zipped past a jumble of red-roofed houses and wild-looking trees, "I've done some pretty impetuous things in my life…" some of them facing a gun "…but never a trip halfway around the world on a few days' notice."

Louisa laughed. "That's because you're a Parker. We're genetically predisposed to planning our steps in advance. My brother was the quintessential one. But every so often, you have to do the opposite, to remind yourself the world's bigger than your to-do list."

She was right about my father and his methodical mind. I closed my eyes, letting the train rock me; she might be right about the rest of it, too.

As we pulled into Circular Quay, the clouds had shifted to reveal blue sky, and the city gleamed ahead of us, the white sails of the Opera House piercing the sky, the Harbour Bridge a dark arch above the water. Louisa squeezed my hand, her own shaking just a little, and I realized I hadn't thought about the office or the caseload or the ticking clock in nearly half a day.

It was only the first morning, and already Australia enchanted me.

* * *

Outside Circular Quay station, the city exploded with

sensory data. Sunlight pinged off high-rise office windows and the steel arc of the Harbour Bridge, and the water below was dotted with ferries in constant motion—each painted in distinctive shades of yellow or green. On a Tuesday morning, the streets simmered with traffic and the clamor of tourists. Every corner seemed engineered for the perfect photo: palm trees, street buskers, the distinctive shape of the Opera House like a precise origami figure against the blue.

Louisa set a pace, navigating through the crowded platform as if she'd lived here for years, pointing out landmarks with the certainty of a local and the flair of a travel agent on commission. "That's the Customs House, now a library. Amazing architecture. Oh! And there's the ferry to Manly Beach, which I booked for Thursday, unless you want to swap with the zoo day?"

I trailed behind, wheeling my suitcase across the uneven pavers, watching as Louisa charmed a street artist into drawing our caricatures in under thirty seconds. I barely registered the result—her eyes were three times too large, and I had the jawline of a movie star—but Louisa clucked her tongue and tipped the artist an extra five for "capturing the spirit."

Outside the train station, we hailed a cab for the last stretch to the hotel. The driver was a silver-haired woman with a voice like sandpaper and opinions on everything from city planning to rugby. "You two new in town?" she asked, glancing in the rearview.

"Visiting from England and the States," Louisa announced. "But my niece is a quick study. She'll know more about Sydney than you by tomorrow morning."

The driver snorted. "Not unless she picks up a proper

accent. They'll eat her alive in Newtown with that American twang."

"Is it that bad?" I asked, suddenly self-conscious.

"Not at all," Louisa said, giving me an approving look. "She's teasing."

We wound through The Rocks, a tangle of narrow streets that looked as if they'd been poured into the cracks between sandstone cliffs. The area was a jigsaw of old pubs, boutiques, and what Louisa called "historic shopfronts," which in reality meant anything built before 1970. Our hotel was tucked between a bakery and a jewelry store, its façade mirrored to reflect the harbor sights.

Inside, the lobby was filled with upscale plush furnishings, a marble tile floor, and the scent of strong coffee wafting from somewhere out of sight. At the front desk, a young man in a navy vest greeted us with a smile that might usually be reserved for royalty or exceptionally good tippers.

Louisa explained that she had checked in already and requested a second key for me.

"Welcome to the Darling," he said. "I see you're booked for two weeks in the Queen Suite, with a balcony overlooking the garden."

Louisa preened. "It's the best room in the place," she told me quietly.

The clerk handed over a card key to me. "Would you like help with your bags? If you'd like a coffee or tea, the lounge is right through there."

While I told him I could manage my one suitcase, Louisa sidled up to the concierge—a woman about my age with a tattooed forearm and a nose ring that glinted in the sun. In less than a minute, Louisa had learned her name

(Jas), her favorite nearby restaurant (Lox & Crumpet, two blocks east), and the best spot for a nightcap (a rooftop bar with "the world's best Negroni" according to Jas's partner).

"Honestly," Jas said, sliding a map across the desk, "if you want to see the real Sydney, skip the bus tours and simply walk. Everything you need is within two kilometers of a train stop, unless you're planning to wrestle a kangaroo."

"No plans for wildlife wrestling quite yet," I said.

Jas grinned. "Give it a day."

Our suite was on the third floor, accessed either by stairs or by an elevator lined with black-and-white photos of the harbor and old city. We had a living room with a curved sofa, dining table, and huge flat-screen. Each of the two bedrooms held a king-sized bed with luxurious linens and a private bath (mine had a round tub standing before wide windows of harbor views—luckily, there were shades). From the living room window, I could see the courtyard below, ringed by ferns and flowering vines, with a single lemon tree at its center.

"Louisa, I can't believe you had enough travel points for a place like this, on top of business-class tickets."

She sent me a cryptic smile and changed the subject. We chatted while I hung my clothes in the closet and set up my laptop on the desk, in case the outside world demanded my attention.

She inquired about Drake and Freckles, which reminded me of how we'd lain in bed, talking into the wee hours, the night I'd said yes to the trip. He assured me that he could indeed take care of the dog, and if a job should come up where she wasn't welcome, he'd confirmed that Gram and Dottie would be happy to watch her (translation: spoil her rotten with treats).

However, in this space, the routines of my real life already felt like a distant echo. I tried to calculate the time difference to New Mexico, couldn't wrap my head around it, and sent texts to both Drake and Ron, letting them know I'd arrived safely and Louisa says hi. When I didn't receive immediate responses, I decided not to stress over it. They would read the messages eventually.

After a quick shower—water pressure like a fire hose, thank you, Australian infrastructure—I found Louisa curled up on the curved sofa, surrounded by an arc of tourist brochures and a legal pad covered in her hasty handwriting.

"Take a look," she said, handing me a list. "I've narrowed it down to the essentials: the Botanic Gardens, Opera House tour, a trip to Manly Beach, and at least one day eating our way through the city. Oh, and the book signing tomorrow afternoon."

I read the list twice. "How many hours of sleep do you think I need to survive all this?"

She ignored the question. "Jet lag is mind over matter, Charlie. If you nap now, you'll be up at three in the morning, watching infomercials about hair removal. Best to get out in the sun and reset your clock."

"Or," I offered, "we could compromise. Walk down to the harbor, stroll around, get coffee, and just people-watch for a while."

She considered this, then nodded with surprising solemnity. "Deal. And let's try out that place Jas recommended for a late lunch."

Outside, the air had warmed, and the streets buzzed with a new shift of humanity. We followed the twists and turns toward the water, Louisa humming under her breath and occasionally stopping to peer into the windows of art galleries and specialty shops. There was no hurry in our steps, and I felt the effort of travel begin to give way to something like curiosity.

At the harbor, we found the café we were seeking, took seats outdoors, and ordered two flat whites. The coffee arrived in cups the color of wet sand, the foam sculpted into careful rosettes. We sipped and watched ferries slice the water, their wakes leaving wriggling lines behind them.

"You know what I love about this city?" Louisa said. "Everyone's moving, but nobody seems to be in a rush. It's like they all know they'll get where they're going, eventually."

I nodded, watching a parade of schoolchildren file past the café, each one in a different-colored hat. We settled in, ordered sandwiches, and felt content to let the world take its own sweet time.

"Do you ever wish you'd settled here instead of Bury St. Edmunds, or any other place you've traveled, for that matter?"

She shrugged. "Every place is just another version of home once you find your rhythm. But it's good to visit the other versions now and then. Makes you appreciate your own."

We lingered until the afternoon sun dipped low enough to paint the Opera House in gold. Another thing about winter—the early sunsets. When Louisa finally stood, stretching like a cat, she patted my arm. "Tomorrow, we'll explore the gardens. And afterwards, we might treat ourselves to a little cake at the Queen Victoria Building. It's world-class shopping, and I've heard it's supposed to be haunted, you know."

I smiled, recalling that she conducted tours of haunted sites in her small hometown. "I thought we were taking a break from ghosts."

She grinned back. "Ghosts can show up, even on holiday, Charlie."

We returned to the hotel in the early gloom, the city lights beginning to be reflected in the harbor, and I found myself looking forward to tomorrow's adventures—despite jet lag and all.

* * *

In theory, a vacation is a retreat—a clearing of the desk and of the mind. In practice, I woke the next morning with a familiar sense of readiness, as if my nervous system hadn't gotten the memo about time off. It was a little past seven when I heard the first trains rattling the city awake. I padded to the window, unsure whether the aches in my legs were jet lag or the residue of yesterday's walking.

Louisa had left a note under my bedroom door: *At breakfast. Come join! Try the lemon curd pancakes. L.* The handwriting was less wild than usual, as if she'd tried to contain her excitement. I dressed in clean jeans and a black T-shirt, then headed down the staircase.

In the dining room, Louisa sat at a table by the window, half turned and chatting up a pair of German tourists who looked alternately bemused and enthralled. When she saw me, she waved me over, motioning for the server to bring another coffee.

"Sleep well?" she asked, and I realized she was in full regalia: a different purple caftan, and this time with a coordinating scarf wound artfully across her shoulders.

"Best sleep I've had in months," I said, ignoring the fact that I had awakened at weird intervals during the night. "You?"

"I did a dawn walk along the harbor," she said. "It's beautiful before the crowds." She lowered her voice, glancing toward the other tables. "Today's the day, darling. I hope you're ready."

"For the Opera House?"

"Well, not exactly. I checked the schedule. The tours are all sold out until Saturday, so I moved us to the next most important thing."

"The book signing? Didn't you say that's a ticketed event?"

"It is, and I did get tickets for us. It's this evening."

"You're really that much into this author?" I tried to imagine Louisa as a fan-girl.

"She's more than a writer. She's an icon—writes those suspenseful stories that'll have you questioning whether to trust anyone in your household. I think *domestic noir* is what they're calling the genre. And besides, she's British. And… I did a writing workshop with her, years ago."

My knowledge of Lily Davenport could be summarized as 'famous' and 'book with blue cover that everyone was reading in the airport.'

"Wait, you did a writing workshop? Were you writing a book?"

Louisa's smile drooped for a second. "Yes, well … I took the workshop and gave it a go. Discovered I don't have the discipline it takes to complete a novel. It's more work than one would think."

I chuckled at her frank admission.

"Lily had a couple of books out, not bestsellers at that point, but you could tell she was going to be something. Before I left England, I saw an article in the *Times* that listed Sydney as a stop on her world book tour, so I thought it might be fun to say hello, you know, see if she remembers the little people."

I got the feeling Louisa remembered this author better than she was letting on, but before I could probe further, she switched the subject.

"You must try these pancakes," she said, sliding her plate toward me. "They have actual lemon zest in the batter. I'm convinced it's medicinal."

I took a bite to humor her, and found myself agreeing. It was a breakfast that could make you apologize to every bowl of oatmeal you'd ever eaten. I ordered a plate of them, too.

We lingered over breakfast, and took a long walk through the botanical gardens, before returning to the hotel for an afternoon of pure relaxation.

Chapter 3

That evening, we dressed for the ticketed book launch gala with the seriousness of soldiers prepping for a parade, though in my case, *dressing* meant swapping my travel jeans for better-fitting black ones and pairing them with the single royal blue sweater I'd brought that didn't double as sleepwear. Donning my black blazer, I paused in the bathroom, eyeing my reflection, and tried to smooth the ends of my hair into something that suggested intention rather than wind-tunnel-aftermath.

Next door, Louisa had gone all out—a sapphire blue dress in her usual flowy style, topped with a paisley scarf so bright it practically vibrated. She emerged into the suite's living room with the certainty of a woman who has never doubted the color wheel.

"You look smashing," she said, eyes twinkling as she

tilted her head in the direction of the door. "You have the look of a woman who might find a crime to solve, even at a literary gala. Very mysterious."

I grunted, but she was halfway down the corridor, scarf trailing behind her like a streamer. She had ordered an Uber and chatted up the driver, who narrated our journey through the city's nighttime arteries. Within ten minutes, we pulled up outside a bookstore that would have made any bibliophile drool: a historic two-story brick building, all glass and glow at street level, the upper story revealing rows of gilt-edged tomes and softly lit display windows. The crowd on the sidewalk seemed to hum with the anticipation of meeting an author they adored.

Inside, the place seemed a sort of church for the literary faithful. Tall, white pillars were up-lit. Stage risers at the far end were flanked by bouquets of indigo and white orchids, mirroring the color scheme of Lily Davenport's current bestseller. Trays of champagne traveled through the crowd in the hands of sleek servers, their dark uniforms matching the midnight blue of the evening sky visible through the front windows.

All of this was, of course, in honor of the author whose photo loomed over the entrance—her signature sharp bob, dark eyes, and a Mona Lisa smile rendered at billboard scale. Posters advertising her new book, *The Fifth Journey,* dotted the walls, and stacks of books had been arranged with surgical precision along every available horizontal surface. It was equal parts book event and a dash of fashion show thrown in. I've attended a few book signings, but none as glammed-up as this one. Evidently, a big publisher will throw big money into events for their star authors.

I stood inside the door, taking in the scene, feeling more than a little bit awed. This was not my natural habitat. The people here—women in cocktail dresses and men in tailored jackets, all sipping from slender flutes and speaking in the conspiratorial tones of those who have never struggled to pay for dry cleaning—looked like they'd stepped off the set of a cleverly written prestige drama. I, the only one in jeans, meanwhile, felt like an understudy in the wrong costume. I looked toward Louisa, who has this natural ability to blend into nearly any crowd, as I'd discovered over the years.

She grabbed a champagne flute and flowed into the crowd with such aplomb that I trailed in her wake like the little rowboat to her party yacht. Most of the others probably assumed I was there as her assistant. Within sixty seconds she'd managed to charm a circle of strangers—one of whom, I gathered, was a poet with three published chapbooks and a partner who "simply lived for the written word." Another was a retired teacher who claimed to have discovered Lily in the wild, "well before she was a blurb on the Booker longlist."

Louisa's talent for learning people's life stories was undiminished by time zones or champagne, and she extracted stories with the skill of a pickpocket. I hung back, eavesdropping on the fragments of conversation that floated my way. I caught a mix of industry gossip ("Did you hear about Ananda's agent? Absolute nightmare."), author-worship ("She signed all three of my books last time. I nearly fainted."), and bits of literary-world braggadocio ("I don't want to sound petty, but isn't this venue a bit—well, provincial for someone of her stature?").

I tried to look like I understood the publishing jargon,

but my eyes kept drifting toward the labeled book sections, thinking I could grab something I hadn't read yet and find an armchair in a quiet corner.

Louisa circled back, cheeks flushed with excitement. "Isn't this wonderful?" she said. "You can feel the energy, can't you? It's like being in a beehive, but with no stings and quality food."

Speaking of which, a waiter swept by, proffering a tray of canapés so artful they looked like something you'd find under a glass dome at a museum. I accepted one reflexively—a baguette slice topped with a perfect rosette of smoked salmon and a small cluster of caviar—then immediately regretted it as the tiny orbs burst in my mouth like a pocket of salt water. I tried not to make a face.

"Try the cheese," Louisa whispered, pointing out another tray. "It's imported. I checked."

We drifted through the store, Louisa stopping every few feet to examine a display or exclaim over a particularly beautiful edition of something she'd read twice. At one point, we passed the poetry section and she recited, from memory, the first four lines of a poem I hadn't thought about since college. "You really do remember everything," I said.

She winked. "It's my curse."

Eventually we made our way toward the rear of the store, where a low dais had been set up for the reading. A sleek, white podium stood at one end, facing an arrangement of chairs half-filled with eager attendees. At the side, a table had been set up with stacks of books for the author to sign and hand out. The air here felt electric—audience members jockeying for position, some clutching copies of the book, others quietly rehearsing the questions they'd ask if given the chance.

I spotted Lily Davenport, flanked by two women who seemed to be part agent, part bodyguard. She wore a simple but striking black dress, and her perfect hair framed her face in a way that made her look both ageless and oddly vulnerable. She was in mid-conversation, but her eyes scanned the room with quick, darting glances.

Louisa leaned in. "Shall we go say hello before it starts, or would that be gauche?"

"I think you can get away with it," I said. "You're the only person in the room not pretending to be cooler than they actually are."

She laughed and led the way, parting the crowd with small apologies. I followed, wishing I'd taken the time to at least iron my blazer.

When we reached Lily, Louisa waited for a natural break in the conversation before she stepped forward with a gentle, "Excuse me—Lily? I'm Louisa Parker, from the Bury St. Edmunds group."

For a nano-second, Lily looked blank, and I braced for an awkward brush-off. When recognition dawned, her entire face reconfigured itself into a smile of genuine warmth.

"Louisa! My God—it's been years!" she said, stepping in to hug my aunt. "You look amazing. You haven't changed a bit."

Louisa glowed. "Neither have you, except for all the fame and fortune. I'm so proud of you."

"Yes, well…" Lily demurred, with a gentle chuckle. "But it's been a wild ride. I never expected half of this."

She turned to me, eyes sharp, and Louisa introduced us.

Lily shook my hand with a dry, steady grip. "Ah yes, the American niece Louisa spoke of. Are you enjoying Sydney?"

"I only arrived yesterday," I said. "But the views are excellent and the people have been so helpful and friendly."

She laughed, turning once more toward Louisa. "You picked a good night to come. At home, I don't normally do events like this. The international tour has been amazing, however. There's often someone from the UK. I think we all migrate in packs."

"Or in search of better weather," Louisa said.

"Or better gossip," Lily countered. "Do you recall my first book signing in Bury, at the Atheneum?"

Even I could envision the scene. The smallish venue was right next to the Angel Hotel, where I had stayed when I visited my aunt. Everything about Bury St. Edmunds and its ancient history made Sydney feel like a brand-new city.

Louisa was chuckling over some shared memory of the signing Lily had mentioned. Apparently, no one but the members of their writing workshop had shown up.

They chatted for a minute, comparing notes on mutual acquaintances in Suffolk, all the while giving the impression that they could easily slip right into their old routines. I stepped back, watching the interplay, and tried to imagine what Louisa was like at my age—more boisterous than now, possibly, but no less intent on making every room she entered more interesting.

A bell chimed somewhere near the stage, and an announcer's voice called the room to order. "If you could all take your seats, we'll start the reading in a few minutes. Please help yourselves to wine and nibbles."

Lily excused herself to confer with the event staff.

Louisa and I drifted to the only two remaining seats in the last row, where the view was slightly obstructed by a display of Seasonal Thrillers, but the acoustics were perfect. I watched as Lily took her place at the podium, scanned the room, and let the silence settle. Then, with a voice honed by her recent years of readings and interviews, she launched into an excerpt from her new book.

The audience was rapt. Even I, who had read the jacket copy with only moderate interest, found myself pulled in by the cadence of her words, the dry wit, and the way she threw in asides that weren't in the text—little self-deprecating jokes that made the entire room lean in closer. At the end, the applause was loud and sincere.

During the Q&A—several people asked about the ending, or about how Lily balanced truth and fiction, or what her next project would be. She deflected that last one with good humor, circling the question but not quite giving a complete answer. I found myself admiring her skill. She was a person who could charm a room while maintaining her personal space.

When it was over, the crowd surged toward the signing table, and for a while the whole place was a tangle of elbows and outstretched books. I hung back with Louisa, watching as people snapped photos, collected autographs, and exchanged breathless commentary. The night outside had gone fully black, but inside the bookstore, the energy felt like it could keep burning until dawn.

Finally, as the crowd thinned and the trays of champagne and canapes disappeared, Lily spotted us and waved us over. "I hope you're not leaving yet," she said. "There's an after-party upstairs. They promised us real food this time."

Louisa's eyes sparkled. "Wouldn't miss it for the world."

I considered making an excuse, but in the end, I followed them up the staircase to the second floor, where the air was thicker, the crowd more intimate, and the conversations less rehearsed. Someone turned on a playlist of old Bowie songs, and a few people clustered around the windows to admire the city lights. Lily circulated with a grace that made this whole thing seem effortless, while Louisa reigned over a corner table, drawing people in with the promise of Lily anecdotes and the occasional impression of an English poet.

I stayed mostly on the perimeter, sipping a Coke and cataloguing the personalities around me: the publishing rep with the nervous laugh, the blogger who never put down her phone, the ex-journalist who seemed determined to argue that every novel was, at heart, a detective story. I didn't disagree, but I was a little too far out of my depth to join in.

At one point, Louisa caught my eye and raised an eyebrow, as if to say, "See? Wasn't this worth the trip?" I smiled back, and finally I found myself relaxing into the moment.

Later, as we finally made our way out into the cool, post-midnight air, Louisa squeezed my arm. "What did you think?"

"Surprisingly tolerable," I said, trying for a straight face. "You should take me to gossipy literary parties more often."

She laughed, and together we rode toward the hotel, the city quiet around us. My jacket was rumpled, but for once, I didn't care.

Chapter 4

The next afternoon, the bookstore planned a more traditional signing, to which we'd been invited by the author herself. We'd spent the morning at leisure in our suite, with a huge room-service breakfast, followed by a venture out, despite threatening skies and the water in the harbor the color of steel. When we made our way to the Harbour Bridge, my feisty aunt spotted a sign advertising a climbing adventure.

"Let's do it!" she said with a tug at my sleeve.

"What—that?" I'd craned my neck to see all the way to the top of the massive arched structure. "No way." I grabbed her hand to keep her back.

"On a sunny day then?" she practically begged.

Yeah, maybe when I was ten and climbed trees like a little monkey. There was no way I was letting my seventy-something aunt tackle such a strenuous activity. I'd aimed a feeble smile at the ticket seller and steered Louisa toward something inland. Distracting her by pointing at a pastry shop had the desired effect.

Now, approaching the bookstore, Louisa was in her element, having spent most of the morning plotting our approach with tactical genius. "We want to avoid the early rush, but not come so late that she's exhausted and desperate for an exit strategy," she'd explained over our coffee and pastry. "I think half past one is the sweet spot."

I nodded, but truthfully, I didn't much care. We'd met Lily the previous evening and Louisa already had her new book. I'm not big on crowds and could have been perfectly content to laze around and read on this overcast day.

At least this group wouldn't be dressed to the nines, and since I was getting talked into it, I might find such a gathering to be a gold mine for people-watching. As a professional observer, that can be a plus.

We arrived as the crowd reached its late-lunch lull. Most of the fans wore either the determined expressions of seasoned line-standers or the shy half-smiles of people who rarely spoke to their idols in person. Lily, seated at the center of the room, managed to look both gracious and alert—shoulders back, pen poised, ready to make each signature feel like a personal inscription despite the probability that she wrote the same sentence a hundred times.

This was a stripped-down version of the previous night's gala. No champagne, no orchestrated lighting. Most of the oversized posters and the showy paraphernalia had been cleared, revealing a much cozier bookshop than I'd first guessed. There was Lily by herself at a signing table with a stack of hardcovers, her name spelled in crisp black letters on a tent card. This, I realized, was the real work of a famous author: long lines of strangers, each expecting a moment of warmth and perhaps a dash of wisdom.

Louisa edged us to the end of the line, her scarf today a cheerful chartreuse meant to defy the gloomy weather. I stood behind her, letting the slow shuffle of bodies bring us closer to the table while I watched Lily at work. Every so often, she'd glance up, scan the next person's face, and adjust her smile—wider for the nervous ones, warmer for the older men, quick and businesslike for the young moms trying to wrangle kids and camera phones.

She handled the books with a kind of reverence, smoothing the title page before she wrote, and never betraying a hint of boredom. But what caught my attention was the way her eyes darted toward the entrance every few minutes—quick, almost imperceptible checks, as if she expected someone else to arrive at any moment.

By the time we reached the front, Lily had signed at least fifty books, but she looked up at Louisa and grinned as if she'd been waiting all day for this. "Well, if it isn't my favorite English rose," she said, and stood to give Louisa a brief, heartfelt hug.

Louisa giggled, a sound I hadn't heard since she took me to a Halloween bakery in Bury St. Edmunds. "You flatter me, Lily. But you're the celebrity now."

"Oh, please. You always had interesting stories." Lily's gaze slid to me, and she cocked an eyebrow in a way that was both playful and, I suspected, faintly challenging. "And how is our American niece today?"

Before I could reply, Louisa jumped in. "My *brilliant* investigator niece. She's solved more crimes than Miss

Marple and probably knows all your plot twists before you actually write them."

I groaned, but Lily laughed. "An investigator …That sounds like a dare. Well, Charlie—do I need to worry about you finding out all my secrets before the sequel's out?"

"Only if you give me a clue," I said, keeping it light. "But honestly, I'm just here for the vacation experience of Sydney."

Lily chuckled. She signed Louisa's book with a flourish, scribbling a quick note on the title page before sliding it across the table. She asked where we were staying, how we were liking Sydney, and whether we'd managed to avoid jet lag. She asked with genuine curiosity, not the perfunctory interest you'd expect from someone moving people through a line.

All the while, she kept those tiny glances toward the front door, never long enough to seem rude, but enough that I started to wonder what—or who—she was expecting.

After a few pleasantries, Louisa pulled out her phone and asked for a photo, which Lily readily agreed to. They posed, heads together, both smiling in a way that was completely unforced.

A few people had come up behind us, but as we turned to go, Lily touched Louisa's arm. "Don't leave right away. I'd love to chat when I'm finished here, somewhere with some privacy."

Louisa's eyes widened. "We'd be delighted."

I let her lead me away from the table, and as we browsed the shelves near the back of the store, I watched Lily sign her way through the last of the queue. Each signature was followed by a small, meaningful exchange—sometimes a sentence, sometimes a laugh or a handshake. She was good, in a way that made me wonder what it cost to maintain that level of grace for hours on end.

When the line finally disappeared, Lily passed her pen to the store manager, who offered her a bottle of water. Lily approached Louisa, the persona of Famous Author briefly replaced by that of Old Friend.

"God, I'm parched," she said. She twisted the bottle cap and took a long drink, then stepped back, letting the façade drop a little.

"So," she said, "I forgot to ask last night, how long are you two in town? I hope you're not leaving before you've seen the real city."

Louisa smiled. "We have ten days left. We've compiled a list of recommendations as long as my arm."

Lily glanced at me, then to Louisa. "Do any of them involve a drink with an old friend in a setting less public than this?" She gave me a quick, conspiratorial wink. "No offense, Charlie, but sometimes the literary world is completely exhausting."

"None taken," I said. "I spend lots of my time hiding from crowds, so I sympathize."

"There's a place I know right around the corner. Quiet, corners to hide in, and the food's better than whatever I might get from room service."

She hesitated for half a second. "Would you both join me? I'll buy the first round. Consider it compensation for whatever trauma Louisa inflicted on you as a child."

"We'd love to." We both said it at once.

Lily laughed, and I noticed again that her smile didn't always reach her eyes. There was something behind it—a wariness, or simply fatigue—that reminded me of clients who showed up at my office with more on their minds than they let on.

As we helped Lily gather her things and made for the exit, I glanced over my shoulder and caught Lily watching the front door as she bade the bookshop staff good afternoon and thanked them. This time, her expression was closer to apprehension than anticipation.

I filed it away as something to ask later, along with the million other things I'd noticed about her over the past hour.

The place Lily led us to was two blocks from the bookstore, a little bar tucked between a dry cleaner and a real estate office, the type of tiny watering hole that disguised its good reputation with a cheap neon sign and blackout windows. Inside, it was almost a different world: dark wood, soft leather, and the right amount of ambient light to make everyone look younger and more attractive. No one here was taking photos or talking about book deals—only a handful of regulars nursing drinks at this hour and ignoring the rest of the universe.

Lily chose a booth in the back, where we could see both the front door and the bartender but were out of sight to most everyone in the place. It was a move that would have made my brother Ron proud, and it confirmed what I'd started to suspect—Lily was a person who valued both privacy and a clear exit.

And she had something on her mind.

As soon as we sat, she relaxed—shoulders down, jaw unclenched, a visible exhale that said more than any polite chatter. "This is better," she said, waving to the bartender for a round. "No offense to the literati, but sometimes you need to be around people who aren't going to ask you about your 'process' or whether you hate your own characters."

The server brought a plate of olives and some kind of savory gourmet popcorn, which Louisa attacked. Lily ordered a glass of a local red. Louisa stuck to white wine, and I requested the red wine. "But one glass only," which earned me a raised eyebrow from both women.

"I'm working on a theory," I explained. "Jet lag plus alcohol equals regrettable karaoke."

Lily snorted. "In that case, we'll keep you hydrated. Somebody has to be responsible."

The wine arrived, and after the first glass, the mood at the table turned slightly giddy. Louisa told a story about her time in Spain, learning flamenco from a man who claimed to have met Hemingway, and I countered with a tale about a failed stakeout in Albuquerque involving a chihuahua and a very persistent meter maid. Lily's laugh was sharp and honest, and she had a knack for punching up our stories with perfectly timed interjections.

Still, beneath the surface, I noticed things: the way she checked her phone, subtly and often, hiding the screen with her hand; the way her gaze darted to the front door every time it opened, then away, as if disappointed or relieved. The way she seemed, at times, to be listening for something none of us could hear.

Even so, she made it easy to forget all that. She told us about her last book tour—a string of airports and chain hotels throughout the UK, punctuated by fans who wanted to discuss her characters' love lives as if they were real people. "I recall a woman in Wales who brought a Tupperware full of scones to every one of my events," she said. "Insisted I take them home, which was sweet, but I had no easy way to carry them along, so by the end of the week my suitcase was a regretful mush that smelled of sugar icing."

She talked about the loneliness of the road, the odd intimacy of sharing secrets with strangers. "I'm not sure who I am half the time," she said. "There's Author Lily, and then there's the person who simply wants to stay in bed and eat room service. I think people like the first one better."

Louisa shook her head. "You underestimate how many people love you exactly the way you are."

Lily smiled, the smile I'd seen at the signing table—bright, professional, slightly distant.

At some point, Louisa excused herself to visit the restroom, and Lily immediately dropped the social pretense. She leaned forward, hands clasped, and looked me dead in the eye.

"Your aunt's a good woman," she said, voice low. "She was self-assured when the rest of us were a mess of nerves over finding the proper agent."

I nodded, unsure where she was going with this.

"You're an investigator, right? Louisa told me you're very good at it."

I tried not to flinch and started to go into the whole explanation about how I'm really an accountant, but that wasn't what she needed to hear. "I do my best."

She looked away, studying her glass. "Do you ever … get a sense, sometimes, that someone's watching you? Or waiting for you to mess up, so they can say, 'I told you so'?"

Doesn't everyone? "All the time," I said, keeping my tone neutral, waiting for the underlying problem to come out.

She smiled, this time a real one. "Figured you'd understand. Sorry. I'm not great at talking about it."

"But you seem to be handling it." Whatever *it* is.

She glanced down at her phone. "Perhaps. Or maybe I'm better at faking it than most."

Louisa returned then, cheeks pink, hair a little mussed. "You two weren't talking shop without me, were you?" she teased.

"Merely swapping anxiety tips," I said. Whatever was bothering Lily, clearly she wasn't ready to fully confide.

We lingered over the drinks, conversation drifting from travel horror stories to our favorite books and back. I almost forgot about the strange tension I'd picked up on earlier, in the bookshop, until Lily checked her phone for the fifth time in ten minutes and muttered, "Not tonight, please," under her breath.

By the time we paid the bill, the bar had filled up with a post-work crowd—not rowdy, but louder, the air heavy with aftershave and perfume. We pushed our way outside, the sudden chill of the evening snapping us awake.

"Tomorrow," Lily said as we stood on the curb, "I want you both to join me for tea at the Windsor. Three o'clock sharp. I have a table booked, and if you haven't tried their scones, you haven't lived."

Louisa beamed. "Charlie, did you hear that? Tea at the Windsor! I can die happy now."

Lily grinned, but when she turned away to hail a cab, I saw her shoulders tense once more. Something was bothering her, probably the thing she hadn't quite got around to telling me earlier. And for reasons I couldn't quite explain, I felt a twinge of responsibility—not only for Louisa, but for Lily, too.

We said our goodbyes and watched her taxi melt into the city traffic.

On the short walk to our hotel, Louisa hummed,

swinging her scarf like a pendulum. "She's wonderful, isn't she?" she said. "I knew she'd be a star."

"She's definitely something," I agreed.

"Do you think she's lonely?" Louisa asked, a trace of genuine concern in her voice. "People think fame is a cure for that, but I'm not so sure."

"I don't think anyone's immune," I said. "Even bestsellers."

Louisa squeezed my arm. "You're wise, you know. I don't tell you that enough."

I smiled. "You do, actually. Every time you talk me into one of your schemes."

She laughed, and we strolled in the comfortable silence.

But that night, lying in my hotel bed with the city's light sneaking around the blinds, I replayed the afternoon. The easy banter, the sudden drops in Lily's mask, the constant vigilance. I knew the signs—a person who believed, with good reason, that their world was two steps away from falling apart. Could be it was nothing but the side effect of living in public for too long. Or maybe it was something else.

Either way, I was looking forward to tea at the Windsor. And, if I was honest with myself, to the puzzle of Lily Davenport.

Chapter 5

If a hotel could be said to take itself seriously, the Windsor certainly did. We stepped into the grand salon at two minutes past three, and it was like walking into a diorama of a vanished era—crystal chandeliers, potted palms that probably outlived several previous owners, plush velvet chairs that threatened to eat you whole if you sank in too deep. The air smelled faintly of lemon oil and scones, overlaid with the brittle sharpness of starched linen. If you believed the photos in the lobby, the place had hosted the Queen Mum, a couple of the Beatles, and several international chess tournaments, all without changing so much as a lampshade.

Louisa navigated the entrance with the sort of confidence only gained by a lifetime of world travel and crashing high teas. She wore a teal dress and a filigree brooch that might double as a lock pick in a pinch. Lily was waiting at a corner table, seated upright as a news anchor, her bob and lipstick perfect.

The table was set for three—silver teaspoons aligned, porcelain gleaming, three-tiered tray awaiting the afternoon's main event. The only other occupant was an upright card bearing our reservation—Davenport Party—rendered in swooping blue calligraphy.

Lily stood, but didn't step forward, offering a quick smile instead of an embrace. If last night she'd been all self-effacing charisma and calculated bonhomie, now I sensed an edge to her movements, a cautiousness she didn't bother to conceal. She greeted us both, her eyes skipping off mine.

"Thanks for coming," she said, smoothing the napkin over her lap. "I know you're on holiday, so I appreciate you indulging me."

Louisa made a dismissive gesture. "Nonsense, darling. You're the toast of the town this week. We're lucky to have you to ourselves for even an hour or so. Besides, the Windsor's tea is legendary. Just try to keep me away from the pastries."

She beamed, but I could tell she was watching Lily with unusual focus, as if keeping a mental tally of every nervous tic. I hadn't said a word to her about Lily's questions to me last evening at the bar.

I slid into the seat next to Louisa, facing the bay windows. Outside, a flowering tree was doing its best impression of spring, though the sky hung with the threat of rain. The tearoom was half full—a few elderly couples, a table of women with almost identical haircuts, and a mother-daughter pair sharing what looked like a birthday.

All innocuous, all chattering away, the teacups clinking in the background. It felt safe, the way hotel restaurants do—expensive, indifferent, and full of people you'll never see again.

A server appeared, his jacket so tight I wondered if he regularly got into the leftover teacakes. He introduced himself as Jonathan, in the rapid-fire cadence of a man who expected to be ignored, and presented the tea list with both hands. The menu was thick enough to be a novel itself, each blend described in reverent detail. Louisa picked something with rose petals and 'overtones of meadow honey.' I went for a basic Assam, reasoning that the purpose of afternoon tea was to act as a pick-me-up. Lily ordered green, no lemon, and when Jonathan repeated it back, her voice caught a little as she said yes.

The server disappeared. We made the usual small talk—how we slept, whether we'd tried the ferry yet, the comparative merits of Australian and English scones ("theirs are smaller but more defiant," Louisa pronounced). Lily was game, but I noticed how she fidgeted with her spoon, spinning it with the tip of one finger. She kept glancing at the mirrored panel behind me, as if using it to check the sightlines to the exit.

After a lull, Louisa tried to raise the mood. "So, have you been mobbed everywhere you go, or only at the book events?"

Lily laughed, but it came out brittle. "Honestly, people are wonderful, but sometimes I wish they came with a mute button. Last week, at the Q&A in Los Angeles, a woman asked if I based my villain on my own mother. In front of two hundred people."

"Did you?" Louisa asked, all innocence.

Lily rolled her eyes. "If only. My mother's far less interesting." But the smile she wore didn't last.

"Speaking of villains," Lily said abruptly, "can I ask you something?" She directed the question at me, but her gaze stayed firmly fixed on the rim of her teacup.

"Of course."

"If someone wanted to scare you," she said, voice low, "but not enough to get caught—what would they do?"

So, here it was, the thing that had been bothering her. It was a loaded question, and I wasn't sure if she meant it as a rhetorical prompt or if she actually wanted an answer. I gave her a noncommittal shrug, hoping she would offer more information.

She hesitated, then opened her purse and withdrew a cream-colored envelope. She set it on the table, palm resting over it for a long moment, before nudging it toward me.

"I got this yesterday," she said. "Well, technically, the front desk delivered it. I assumed it was from my publisher, but there was no return address. It's addressed only to 'Ms. Davenport, c/o Windsor Hotel.'" She gave a tight smile. "Inside was a note. No threats, no crazy rants, but … creepy. Too formal. Like someone was trying to sound clever, or important."

"Do you mind?" I asked, gesturing to the envelope.

"Please," she said, relief clear in her posture.

I peeled it open. The paper was heavy, off-white, and folded twice, a kind of stock reserved for wedding invitations or pre-lawsuit correspondence. The note was written in real ink—fountain pen, judging by the tiny halos around the upstrokes. Elegant handwriting but inconsistent, the sort that came from someone trying to disguise their natural style.

It read:

Dear Lily,

Your journey has been most entertaining.

Do you still remember the promises made under that August sky?

Some debts cannot be erased by distance, or by fame.

Only by acknowledgment.

There will be more. Await instructions.

A.

Nothing else. No demand, no threat, no signature. Simply the letter A.

I passed the note to Louisa, who read it twice and clucked her tongue. "That's not a fan letter," she said, laying it flat for all of us to see. "It's a ... I don't really know. Who's A?"

Lily looked at her hands. "I have no idea. I mean, I know lots of people with an initial A. In publishing, everyone's an initial. But the wording..." she trailed off.

"There's more to it, isn't there?" I didn't want to pry, exactly, but I'm not good with games of coyness.

Lily nodded, her mouth compressed. "I got similar notes in London, New York, LA, and—believe it or not—Honolulu. They're not identically worded, but the tone is the same. Like someone's following me from city to city, keeping a tally." She glanced up and quickly jammed the note back into her bag.

Jonathan returned with our tea, artfully avoiding any eye contact. He poured for us all, set down the teapots, and retreated. Only after he left did Lily continue, dropping her voice lower.

"The first one, in London, I ignored. Assumed it was

some weird inside joke from a friend. The second was in New York, and it mentioned something I'd said in a podcast—the way I phrased a line about 'debts and destiny.' After that one, I started taking them a bit more seriously."

"Have you told anyone?" I asked.

She sighed. "I've tried. The hotel security in New York said they'd check the cameras, but of course there was nothing—they claimed they found the envelope with my name on it at the concierge desk. In LA, the guy at the front desk felt sure the note came via regular post, but it had no postmark. My agent says I'm overreacting, and my publisher thinks it's some viral marketing campaign by a rival. But it's not. It's personal. Whoever it is, they know my schedule. They know exactly where I'm staying, even when I've experienced travel delays."

Louisa reached across the table and squeezed Lily's hand. "That's awful, darling. Did you keep all the notes?"

Lily nodded, pulling a slim folder from her purse. "I didn't want to carry them around with me, but I was afraid to leave them in my room. Here. Don't worry about leaving fingerprints. They've all been handled by multiple people, at this point." She slid it across to me, her hands shaking enough to make the transfer clumsy. I opened it and spread out the small pages.

The paper was of good quality; I knew that much. I took time to read each one twice. The wording was odd—literate, but not the way most people speak. Each contained a few lines of prose and was signed with a single initial, the letter A. The handwriting appeared to be identical.

The Sydney note was the most verbose, the most direct. I put them in sequence, feeling the escalation in each one—not in their words, but in the tone. The phrase 'under that

August sky' sounded almost romantic, but following it with a reference to debt. I didn't get the impression this was meant to woo Lily.

"It sounds like whoever sent these believes they were owed something, and that you would know what it is," I suggested. "Could they have come from a …"

"Lover? It's been way too many years since I've had one of those in my life. My work is my only passion these days."

Louisa took a sip of her tea, scanned the notes, brow furrowed. "It's like a stalker, but not a romantic one," she said. "There's no longing. Only … judgment."

Lily nodded, looking close to tears, but she kept her voice steady. "That's what scares me. This isn't a fan who wants to meet me, or someone who's in love with a character. It's like a critique, but for my life."

"Has anyone approached you during the tour? I mean, other than everyone who wants a book signed?"

She fidgeted in her chair and became intent on picking at a cuticle.

"It would help me to know everything."

She looked up. "Twice, out on the streets, I swore someone was following me. In London, I disregarded it. That's my home territory, and it was a safe neighborhood. In New York, there was definitely a man who followed my moves for several blocks one evening after I'd finished having dinner and was walking back to my hotel. It was a bit unnerving."

Louisa reached over and took her hand. "Oh, dear. It certainly would be. Did he speak to you or, heaven forbid, try to touch you?"

"No, nothing like that. I reached the safety of the

lobby and he walked on by. I felt sure I was simply jittery after receiving the two notes. I did mention to my publicist that I'd appreciate an escort in each of the other places, and they have graciously provided that."

I glanced around the room, scanning faces, but nothing looked out of place. "Did you tell anyone else? Friends, old colleagues?"

Lily picked at the crust on an exquisite little sandwich. "As I mentioned, other than trying to learn more from hotel security, I've spoken only to my editor and publicist."

"What about in other parts of your life, is there anyone who might have an axe to grind?"

"I keep to myself, mostly. There are a few writers I've had disagreements with over the years, but nothing that would make someone fly around the world to harass me. Nobody I know would do this."

"Do you want to go to the police?" Louisa asked, her tone gentle.

"I tried," Lily said, barely above a whisper. "They said there's nothing illegal about letters, or in walking down a street. Unless it's an actual threat, it's not considered stalking. I'd have to be attacked before they'd take it seriously." She looked at me, eyes raw. "Sorry, I didn't mean to dump this on you. I ... I didn't know who else to ask."

Louisa glanced at me, her eyes asking a question she didn't say out loud. I answered with a tiny nod—yes, I was interested. Yes, I would help, even if all I had to offer was a pair of eyes and a suspicious mind.

"Can I keep these?" I asked, tapping the folder. "For a day or two. I'll scan them and see if I can pick up anything."

Lily looked relieved, then mortified. "God, yes, of course. I'm so sorry. This was supposed to be fun. We were going to have tea and cake, and here I am making it all about me."

"Nonsense," Louisa said, patting her hand tenderly. "You did the right thing. You're not alone. Charlie is brilliant at these things. If anyone can solve it, she can."

I felt a familiar surge—equal parts protectiveness and the electric buzz of a new mystery. "If you want," I said, knowing now why she'd watched the exit doors so intently, "I can stick with you at the next event. See if anyone stands out. We can also talk to people at the hotel, look at the delivery logs, talk to the security staff, get the lay of the land."

Lily nodded, her posture softening. "That would help. Quite a lot."

We drank our tea, picking at the pastries with more curiosity than hunger. Outside, the sky darkened a shade, hinting at rain. The room's noise had faded, the other guests gone or lost in their own stories. The three of us formed a strange, intimate triangle—one woman scared, one trying desperately to comfort her, and me, already searching for the answers.

As we rose to leave, Lily smiled—a real one this time, if a little shaky. "Thank you both."

We stepped into the marble hall, the echoes of our shoes sounding in the large space. I tucked the folder into my bag.

Vacation was officially over and I couldn't wait to get started.

* * *

I'd forgotten how quickly muscle memory takes over.

One second you're a tourist, blinking at pastries, and the next you're parsing the world into suspects, patterns, and clues. I barely remembered walking from the hotel entrance to the curb; I was replaying the conversation, shuffling the notes in my mind.

Back in our suite, Louisa changed from her fancy dress into comfy pants and a warm tunic, an edge against the chill of the day outside.

"Do you want a proper drink?" she asked, halfway to the minibar. She uncapped a miniature bottle of sherry and poured us each a tiny bit, which seemed perfectly in character for her.

I sat down, gave the notes a once-over, then a twice-over, looking for what my brother called "the thing that doesn't fit the suit." Each note was written in the same hand—elegant, but with the tiniest jitter on the left-leaning diagonals, like someone whose patience wore thin at the bottom of every downstroke. The paper was consistent: heavy, unlined, and uniformly cut, all five sheets a very British A5 in size. No letterhead. Only the faintest watermark when held to the light. Blue ink, written with bitter intent.

As I read, the more I recognized the rhythm of obsession. Whoever wrote these had studied Lily's career, and her tour, with the attention to detail of a stalker or a superfan—or someone with a professional stake in her downfall.

Louisa hovered behind me, her silence an unspoken question. "What do you think?" she said finally.

"I think someone wants to remind Lily of something, but I can't tell what. The message seems to be about instilling guilt, but there's no substance. A good threat is specific, or at least personal—this is a series of pointed reminders that she owes a debt." I looked up and found Louisa's eyes on me. "Whoever A is, they're escalating. The first notes are sort of poetic, but this last one is close to gloating."

Louisa chewed her lip. "Do you think she's in danger?"

I hesitated. "It doesn't read like an assassination prelude, but people escalate when they're not satisfied. I'd like to be at Lily's next event, see who shows up." I was reminded of the way Lily seemed watchful at each of her public appearances. "And I'll talk to the hotel staff—concierge, delivery desk. Somebody must have handled these envelopes, even if it was to set them aside. Someone at the Windsor may have seen who dropped off this most recent one."

Louisa smiled. "I knew you'd take it seriously."

"Old habits," I said, tucking the envelopes into the folder. "We should call Lily, ask for a list of everywhere she'll be this week. No point in waiting for this person's next move."

Louisa didn't object. She poured another sherry, handed it to me, and sat down with her own. "You're very astute, you know."

I shrugged. "Sometimes it's easier to see other people's patterns than your own."

Chapter 6

A sheet of expensive paper and a matching envelope lay on the desk. The woman picked up her pen and unscrewed the cap, re-reading her latest message to the author she'd once idolized. Why did some writers get all the recognition while others received none?

She gritted her teeth, recalling the book signing a few weeks ago in London. While she sat at the back of the room, Lily Davenport gave her pretty little talk, complete with exactly the right number of self-deprecating comments. Not too full of herself, giving her adoring fans the right amount of love. Not a clue to the audience that this author had received a disquieting note this very morning.

Lily Davenport had been an excellent leader in the series of writing workshops, giving valuable tips, and insightful feedback. The participants loved her. *Darling*

Lily. Sweet Lily.

The woman actually let out a growl.

So, why had her own work not been widely accepted? She pawed through pages of notes that lay scattered across the desk. The battered sheets in her notebook attested to the fact that she'd studied hard, had truly worked at her craft. Her written work was surely as good as Davenport's.

She looked up, catching sight of her own face in the mirror above the desk. Her mouth was pinched in a tight, downward frown. Did Lily deserve literary success because her smile was nicer? No, she decided with a grimace toward her reflection.

She glanced over at the tattered copy of her one published novel, bile rising as she recalled the publisher's regretful decision that they could not spend the money to publish another. The first simply had not sold well enough, and they most certainly would not pay her, not even a few hundred pounds as an advance for a second book. Sorry.

Sorry. The word rankled.

Well, this wasn't over yet, and Lily Davenport would pay.

She took a deep breath, reread the words she'd penned on the creamy page, and steadied her hand as she added her signature initial—*A*.

Chapter 7

We met Lily at the Museum of Sydney the next morning, where the author was to sign books for the gift shop's stock. She arrived flanked by two publishing staffers—one carrying a stack of books, the other wielding a phone and a nervous smile.

Lily's staff peeled off when they reached the café near the front entrance, giving us an hour of unsupervised access. She wore sunglasses and a scarf, although the sun barely broke through the clouds. She ordered a latte, sipped half of it, then pushed the cup away.

"Thank you for yesterday," she said. "And for ... not laughing."

"Why would we laugh?" Louisa asked.

"Because it sounds mad. Like something you'd hear on a bad true-crime podcast. I haven't slept properly in weeks, and my creative process is rubbish. I'd hoped to write the opening chapters of my next book during this tour, but—" She gave a tiny, hopeless gesture.

I asked if she had brought a copy of her itinerary, as I'd requested last night. She slid the page over to me.

"Help me put together a picture. Did anyone unusual approach you at the last few signings? Anyone lingering too long, or showing up more than once?"

She thought for a minute, her mouth pursed. "The crowd is normally very similar. Lots of women, many younger and quite a few my age, some older men who ask about my research, a few students. Nobody's thrown me off. Selfies are popular, but rarely do I get anyone's name other than a request to inscribe a book."

I made a note of it, though it felt like a dead end. "What about at your hotels? Has anyone tried to contact you in person or reappeared in more than one place?"

"The tour keeps us moving—different hotels and signing venues in every city, all booked by the publisher and coordinated with escorts in each place. I usually don't know the exact itinerary until I check in and get a printout. Sometimes we use my full name at the hotel, sometimes a variation. But the notes are waiting for me when I arrive."

"Same envelope, same paper?" I asked.

"Always," Lily said. "It's creepy. Like someone's inside the system."

Louisa cut in. "Did any of the notes mention something only you would know? A private detail, or a secret from your past?"

Lily hesitated, then pressed her palms to her eyes. "Perhaps. The bit about 'debts and destiny' was a line I used in a podcast interview, but it's not as though it was private. The rest is all veiled, like they want me to guess at the answers, as if it's a game and I'm meant to lose. I've gone through names in my head and I can't think of anyone who would do this. And the initial A is so common it means nothing."

I filed it away. "Have you tried talking to the publisher's publicity department, or whoever handles your travel? Could someone on their staff be compromised?"

She made a noise halfway between a laugh and a sob. "I did. They think it's a prank, or a stunt by a fan. My publicist told me to use it as marketing—'Nothing sells like danger,' she said." Lily glanced up, her eyes shining in the gray light. "I feel like I'm the only one who's actually unnerved by this."

I considered that. "If it is a stunt by a fan, I would think they'd show themselves. It seems that type of behavior is more about them than about you … Any ideas on that?"

She merely shook her head.

"If it's okay," I said, "I'd like to check the hotel records. See if the notes were dropped off in person or by courier. We may be able to catch someone on CCTV."

Lily nodded. "The page I gave you includes my travel itinerary. There's another event tonight—a library reading with Q&A afterwards, nothing formal. If you're there, it could be that you'll spot something I missed."

I let the conversation drift after that, letting Lily's nerves unwind with each minute of normality. We talked about other things—the architecture, the variety of birds here, the fact that Australian ice cream shops had more vegan options than any city in America. But the tension lingered below the surface.

A few minutes later, Lily's publicity staffers returned. "I'd better go inside and speak with the gift shop crew and sign those books. It was nice of them to agree to stock a novel that isn't about Sydney history."

The two young women stood aside as we rose, and Louisa gave Lily a hug. "We'll see you at the library later."

* * *

I spent the remainder of the morning at the Windsor Hotel, perfecting my story as to my reasons for wanting to know about personal messages received by one of their guests. By the time I made it past the desk clerk and the concierge, I had it down well enough to speak with someone in hotel security. Unfortunately, the young man was fairly new on the job, the type who probably didn't utter a word without the permission of his boss.

Louisa, acting as a friend of Lily's, tried a few questions on the maids in the upstairs corridors, but these employees, too, had obviously been coached on the perils of speaking to strangers.

"I'd hoped to get access to the security office," I told my aunt when we met on the street thirty minutes later. "Surely in a place this size there are lobby cameras that would show someone handing off a note or dropping it off at the desk."

"One would think so," she agreed.

"I did get a business card, so I'm hoping the security chief will be in later. If I call in advance, I hope he will actually agree to see me."

"Don't give up, Charlie. If direct contact fails, I'm sure you can convince Lily to go with you. As an important guest, she'll carry some clout."

We began walking, up a steep hill, past a jumble of art

galleries and gift shops selling koala plushies and twenty-dollar boomerangs. I thought of looking for gifts to take home to Ron's kids, but they'd all outgrown plushies long ago, and I've learned from experience that taking home something from a place the recipient has never been … the items usually end up stuffed into the back of a closet somewhere.

We found lunch, sushi handrolls, which we ate on a park bench in a welcome spot of sunshine. Only minutes later, I caught myself yawning. I wasn't unhappy when Louisa suggested that since the evening might run late, an afternoon nap might be in order.

She was correct. I felt considerably refreshed when I woke, astounded to see that I'd slept well over two hours. I found Louisa in the living room of our suite, a bottle of wine and a cheese plate at hand.

"Where did you—?"

She merely smiled and poured me a glass. "We'll need a bit of sustenance, my dear. We leave for the library in less than an hour."

We got an Uber. The night had turned blustery, the wind cutting, and it would have been over a mile to walk.

I positioned myself near the entrance inside the library, blending in with my jeans and casual jacket. The crowd seemed typical—book lovers, retirees, a couple of bored teenagers, and a handful of local press. Lily would arrive with her escorts, do the reading, answer questions, and sign books at a table by the door. I watched every face, every movement throughout the program, but I didn't spot any viable suspects.

Halfway through the Q&A, a hand shot up near the back. The man was unremarkable—thirty-ish, brown hair, wire-frame glasses, plain jacket. "You write a lot about memory in your stories," the man said. "Do you ever worry about misremembering? Or about people who remember things differently than you do?"

Lily froze for a second. "I think all writers worry about that. Sometimes the act of writing is simply trying to put order to the chaos of ideas in your head."

The man sat down, not seeming satisfied with the answer, but he didn't ask anything else. He lingered only a few minutes before edging his way out of the row and leaving the library without looking back.

I pretended to snap a selfie, surreptitiously making sure his face was in the background. He seemed like a nobody, but in my business, you never know what minor facts will end up being important.

Afterward, Lily thanked us again for coming, her exhaustion showing through the makeup and the careful hair. To my question about whether she recognized the man who'd asked the unusual question, she said no.

"If I get another note, I'll call," she said, clutching her coat around her. "I wish I could figure out what they want."

"We will," I said, hoping I sounded more confident than I felt.

Back at the hotel, Louisa and I debriefed. "You think it's the man from the library?" she asked.

"She didn't know him, but he didn't seem to want anything but to pin her down with an awkward question. I couldn't tell whether he was truly invested in the answer or not. He could also be a decoy, someone enlisted by the sender of the notes. He's the first one who seemed interested in the real Lily, not only her books."

Louisa poured the last of the sherry. "Might be he's a

fan who went sour."

I shrugged. He hadn't seemed angry or bitter, and his only suspicious move was that he left before getting a book signed.

"Or a rival," she said. "Or an ex-friend. Or a family member of one of those."

In other words, it could be nearly anyone. However, in the category of ex-friends or rivals, surely Lily would have recognized such a person. "We'll find out."

She raised her glass. "To the mystery, then."

I clinked mine to hers, and we drank.

But as I went through the motions, I kept thinking of the note-writer's words. *Some debts cannot be erased by distance, or by fame. Only by acknowledgment.*

I needed to find out who was owed, and for what.

And, if possible, before the next city on the tour.

Chapter 8

I'd found that the best time to study a crime scene—or in this case, the artifacts of a campaign of psychological warfare—was not in the moment of discovery, but in the lull that followed. It's in the hush after the initial discovery that patterns start to surface, and details admit they've been hiding in plain sight all along.

Louisa had decided to take advantage of the spa at our hotel the next afternoon, but I wanted to go over the notes with Lily and get her recollections about the delivery of each. We would meet up for dinner later.

Lily's suite at the Windsor was as good a temporary lab as any. The air smelled of hotel soap and new carpet, overlaid by the faintest trace of dried rose from the housekeeping sprays. Past the full-length windows clouds moved across the sun, but in here the lighting was gentle and unhurried. Lily had drawn the curtains against the glare, and the lamps gave off a golden, faux-firelight glow. It felt like a place where one would find the solution to a conspiracy.

Instead, we had a stack of anonymous notes and a month's worth of questions.

"I'd like to go over these again," I suggested, once we'd settled into opposite corners of the room's low couch, an elliptical coffee table beside us. I'd brought the folder containing the five threatening notes and my own legal pad, for notetaking, but for the moment I watched Lily, measuring her mood.

"I keep second-guessing myself, wondering if this is nothing," she said, but the shake in her hand made a lie of the statement. "You know how it is. You get a weird vibe and suddenly everything's a clue."

"Sometimes the vibe's the only real clue," I said gently.

She set down her teacup as I opened the brown folder. There were the five notes inside, each folded twice and tucked into its own separate envelope. I watched her hands as she picked up each one and arranged them in a tidy line. "This is the order in which I received them."

I'd spent the entire morning researching papers and inks, so I started with the first envelope in the sequence.

London:

The paper was heavy, possibly Crane Crest or something close, cut to precise A5 dimensions. A single sheet, folded twice. The ink was midnight blue, old-school, probably Waterman—per my best guess while researching all this.

The handwriting slanted slightly left, every capital more ornate than the last. The note was brief and I read it aloud:

"You look radiant from a distance, but the closer one gets, the

more shadows appear. Be honest, for once in your life.
A."

I ran my gloved finger along the top edge, feeling for any ridge or flaw, as one of my online experts had suggested. There were none. I held it to the light—the same faint watermark, the density of quality rag.

"The threat here seems to be someone who believes you're basically dishonest, Lily. Can you think who that would be?" I knew she had given this a lot of thought, but I gave her several minutes.

When she had no answer, I placed the note flat and moved to the next, the one from New York.

"Your voice carries here. Old debts are not paid by silence.
A."

"Same paper. Same ink. Handwriting identical except for a barely perceptible tightening of the script. As though the writer started rushing, or perhaps grew impatient. This one refers to old debts, so I'll pose the question again. Does that ring any bells for you?"

As before, she gave a sad shake of her head. "My brother thought I owed him five quid I'd borrowed in primary school. Brought it up numerous times, until our mum reminded him that it was I who'd loaned him the money." The moment of levity brightened her mood for a second.

I checked the envelope for any impression—nothing. The glue on the flap had been moistened cleanly, and it had no other identifying features. I set that one aside and picked up the next.

"Do you fear that the past might catch up, or do you simply hope it forgets you? Some things will not stay buried, even under the

California sun.

A."

This one was crisper. The lines on the fold were severe, and the ink had pooled in a spot at the end. The question at the top was not rhetorical, although the sender pretended otherwise.

"The message fits with what you suggested about it being someone from my past," Lily touched the note cautiously. "But I'm at a loss as to who that would be."

Moving on to Honolulu:

"Paradise is only a mask. You of all people should know the rot beneath.

A."

The text was nearly poetic, but by this point, the script had taken on a new tempo—almost angry, the loops in the As opening up when the pen was being pushed harder. "It reminds me of the way people start to lose their patience when waiting for someone to catch up to their point," I suggested.

Lily didn't disagree, but she seemed baffled as to the meaning. I replaced it and picked up the final note, which she'd received here in Sydney.

"Your journey has been most entertaining.

Do you still remember the promises made under that August sky?

Some debts cannot be erased by distance, or by fame.

Only by acknowledgment.

There will be more. Await instructions.

A."

I set the final note down with a sigh. "We have the idea repeated that there's a debt of some kind. The escalation seems clear enough with the last line. Whoever wrote these set out to unsettle you, not threaten—at least not in the physical sense. But there's a line in the latest one that stayed with me. *Do you still remember the promises made under that August sky?* It's unusual, and I'm trying to guess what meaning it holds for whoever sent it."

I glanced up at Lily, who had been watching my face as if I might involuntarily blurt out the answer to everything if she stared long enough.

"Does that phrase mean anything to you, other than the fact that it's August now?" I asked.

She shrugged. "Not specifically. I've done other book launches in August, but don't recall the sky as a memorable part of them. My birthday is in winter. Unless they're talking about… you know, a metaphorical sky."

I set that thread aside and went to my next question. I picked up my notebook and flipped to a clean page. "Mind if we run through the deliveries? The physical stuff. Where, when, who handed it to you? That sort of thing."

Lily nodded.

"London first," I said. "How did you receive the envelope?"

She squinted at the table, searching for details. "I was at the Clarion—old hotel, heavy carpets everywhere. I checked in early, went out for a walk, returned to the room, and found it had been slipped under the door. No name on it, only 'Ms. Davenport.' The envelope was pristine—clearly it had not traveled through the post."

"You had no staff interaction?"

"None. With the sentence about looking radiant, I assumed it was from a fan. I don't know. I nearly threw it in the bin at the time."

I scribbled a note. "And New York?"

Lily's voice steadied. "The Warwick. That time it was waiting at check-in when I arrived. I'd come directly from a signing, so my head was buzzing. The envelope was tucked with my room keys—like it was standard mail. The woman behind the counter said, 'You have a message,' and handed it to me."

"It came exactly like this? Not inside a larger envelope with a return address?"

"No. It was identical to the London one—as you see it here."

"Did you ask any questions of the hotel staff?"

"Not really. As I said, I was tired at the end of a very long day. I tossed the envelope into my bag."

I stared at my notes, took a long breath. "Okay, Los Angeles?" I prompted.

"That one was different. The event was at the publisher's retreat in the hills. I checked into my accommodations late and was handed a note: Please phone room service. I assumed the hotel had sent a welcome package, maybe fruit or wine. The staffer—I think his name was Josh?—said, 'This was dropped off for you earlier today,' and left before I could ask anything. But the room service tray held only the envelope and a bottle of water."

"Was it sealed?" I asked.

"Yes. The paper and envelope looked like it had come out of a fresh box. No fingerprints or smudges, at least none I could see." She fidgeted in her seat. "This time I felt a bit unnerved. Three cities, three matching envelopes. I phoned down to the hotel manager, who promised to look into it. But by the next day she reported that no one recalled where the envelope had come from. I told my publicist and editor. They seemed duly concerned, but couldn't offer any solutions."

I could see Lily was getting tired, but felt I needed to press on. "And Honolulu?"

"Room service, but this time a woman. She wore one of those flower leis, and she handed me the envelope directly. When I opened it, the paper was cold. As if it had been refrigerated."

"Odd."

"After Honolulu, I began to seriously consider that perhaps this person is traveling with me. Keeping close, but not close enough to be seen." Lily's eyes mirrored the fear in that possibility.

I pointed to the row of envelopes. "And here, in Sydney?"

She glanced at the coffee table. "Here it was delivered by a junior concierge. Tall, with a nervous tic—he kept clearing his throat. He knocked on the door, handed me the envelope, and left before I could tip him."

"You have quite a memory for details. Did you get his name?"

"Robbie, I think his name badge said?"

I wrote the name in the margin. "So, other than in London, someone physically brought the notes to you. Not by mail, always by hand."

"Yes. And usually either before an event or shortly after."

I nodded, considering the psychology. "It's about revealing their presence—about making you doubt yourself as you're about to appear in public. It's something of a classic stalker strategy, but done with restraint."

She leaned back, tucking herself into the corner of the sofa protectively.

"Do you want to take a break?"

"Let's cover as much as we can now."

I flipped the page and drew a quick grid, blocking out the dates and cities, overlaying Lily's tour schedule from her publisher's website.

"What's your next event?" I asked, not looking up from my notes.

She took a shaky breath. "I have a day off, then there is the Harbour Street Fair, and a signing at a small shop. The street fair is at noon on Saturday. It's an open-air thing—lots of people, some local press, but mostly readers. I believe some other authors will also be signing. I'll be at a tent with a stack of books and my pen."

"And after that?" Her schedule sounded grueling.

"There's a private publisher party. Sunday night, at a restaurant on the waterfront. They're inviting local media, some VIPs, but it's supposed to be a closed list."

I wrote it down, boxing the dates in black ink. Something kept eating at me. "If someone wanted to intimidate you, why bother following you across continents instead of waiting for you at home, mailing them to you?"

Lily pressed her lips together, before she answered. "If they knew my home address, they might. But my publisher is quite strict about privacy. The event venues are public knowledge—fans look up the events, journalists get press packets. It's not hard to figure out. But I don't think my hotels are revealed through those means."

"So, it's not a crank with a mailing list. This is someone who's following your route, researching your appearances in advance, keeping tabs on every move you make. The fact that a note arrives in each city makes me think it's all about intimidation. They want to throw you off your game, watch you stumble."

"Unless ... thinking aloud now ... perhaps the person mails each of the notes ahead to my hotel, enclosed in a larger envelope, with instructions for hotel personnel to be certain I receive it." Her expression brightened. "That could mean the writer of the notes is not actually traveling my route."

I gave that some thought, wanting to match her optimism. "The only issue I see with that is, according to one of the delivery persons, the envelope was dropped off by someone in person. And none of them mentioned it arriving in the mail or by courier service. Do I have that right?"

Lily's smile faded. She drew her knees up to her chest, arms folding tight across her ribs, and looked like she wanted to shrink to the size of a postage stamp and disappear through the mail slot.

"You're right." Her voice was quieter than before. "Does it help, knowing that much?"

"I think so," I said. "It gives me a series of questions to ask. I'm planning to get out tomorrow and ask questions, interview hotel employees who actually handled the note, if I can. I'd appreciate it if you'll call the head of security here at the Windsor and authorize him to cooperate with me."

She nodded agreement, her eyelids drifting downward. "After the events here in Sydney, I'm off to Rome, the last city on the tour. There's only one event, at the National Library, and a news interview of some kind."

We both mulled over everything we'd discussed.

"One other thing," I said, breaking the silence. "Circling back, have you recalled any part of your past—

school, family, old friends—that you think this could tie to? Anyone who might want to unsettle you, not for fame but for something personal?"

Lily opened her eyes, and a brief flash of anger showed beneath the fatigue. "I've thought about that, whether there was some old conflict. But everyone who came to mind is either dead, in another hemisphere, or so estranged I doubt they know I'm alive. I keep asking myself: what debt? What promise? If it's meant to scare me, it's working. But if it's meant to get me to confess—well, I can't confess to an action I don't remember."

I nodded. "People who want an admission like that usually escalate. They crave an audience."

"So, what's next?" she asked.

I closed my notepad with a decisive snap. "At the event tomorrow, I'll be there to watch the crowd—focus on people who seem more interested in you than in the books. I'll also pay special attention to anyone who looks vindictive, or angry, or like they're counting down to something." Or the thirty-ish, brown-haired man who'd asked the oddball question the last time. I hated to admit it, but he was really my only suspect at the moment.

Lily smiled, the tension in her shoulders relaxing barely enough to notice. "You're good at noticing things."

"Invested people make mistakes," I said, gathering the notes and stowing them in their folder. "And I like giving them the opportunity."

Lily smiled, but the anxiety didn't leave her face. "You make it sound so ... procedural. As if it's another case to tick off the list."

"It is another case," I said, closing the folder. "But it's *your* case, so it matters greatly."

She sat back, blowing out a long, shuddery breath. "Can I ask you something?"

"Sure."

"How do you keep from taking it home with you?" She gestured at the folder. "All this hate, or fear, or whatever it is."

"Practice," I said, and meant it. "And I have a good spouse who makes me stop working after a certain hour. You get used to compartmentalizing. And when you can't, you call in favors and trust the people who know you best. That's how you keep from going nuts." It sounded good, and I hoped it reassured her.

For a long moment, the only sound was the faint whir of the hotel's heating system. I thought of Drake at home, wondered what he was doing. I'd try to coordinate a phone call later.

Lily straightened. "Thank you," she said. "Not only for the detective work. For taking it seriously."

I smiled, but kept my voice light. "That's what I do. And I promise we'll get to the bottom of it before Rome. It's possible the stalker is planning something there, a grand finale or something, and I'd like to stop them here in Sydney, before it comes to that."

As I left her suite, I caught my own reflection in the mirrored wall by the elevator—hair pulled back, jaw set, eyes skipping past the moment to the next set of clues.

In the Windsor lobby, I phoned Louisa and we agreed to meet at a tiny Thai restaurant near our hotel, where we indulged in curry and noodles until we were both stuffed. I filled her in on the plans for the remainder of the week and asked for her help in surveilling the crowd at each event, looking for our stalker. Her face lit up at the chance to help.

Whoever *A* was, they thought they were in control. But if they were invested enough to cross an ocean and track Lily city by city, they'd already made their first real mistake.

While it was true that we'd have a devil of a time placing any one person in the same cities at the same time as Lily—the sheer number of flights made that nearly impossible, at least without a name to track—we had some slight advantage. They thought nobody was watching the watcher.

But we were.

Chapter 9

Enough. I woke with the resolution to do something besides stare at the collection of notes Lily had received. Today I would get out and do some old-fashioned canvassing to see what I could learn about the person who'd been frightening one of the world's favorite authors.

Louisa had stayed up late to finish reading Lily's book, and I knew she wouldn't care if I skipped out early. I left quietly and made my way the few blocks to the Windsor Hotel. Office workers in smart outfits poured out of the train station, single-minded in their trek to their desks in the surrounding high-rise buildings. I walked into the Windsor, again impressed with its opulence.

At the front desk, a young man with an immaculate part and a suit that probably cost less than it appeared looked up. His name tag read "Eric J."

"Good morning, how may I help you today?"

I gave him the smile that has gotten me out of more than one speeding ticket.

"I'm here on behalf of your guest, Ms. Lily Davenport." I let the name hang, watching for recognition. I got it in less than two seconds. "I'm her private investigator. There's a situation with the delivery of an envelope to her suite."

"Ah." His smile lost two watts of intensity. "Let me see if our guest services manager is available."

Within two minutes I was seated across the huge cherry wood desk of an Adam Welles. At a glance I knew he was accustomed to dealing with a wealthy clientele. I outlined the basics: a famous guest had received a series of anonymous notes, including one delivered here at the Windsor on the day she'd checked in.

"I'd like to see the security video for that day. I hope we can identify someone dropping the note—"

He gave me an apologetic look, one shoulder raised slightly. "I'm sorry, but we have a very strict policy—"

"I know the policy, but we're a little past that. This is a matter of legal interest and guest safety, which Ms. Davenport has hired me to look into. She said the threatening note came to her via concierge staff, but the envelope lacked both a return address and a verifiable courier record."

Welles's lips compressed to a colorless line. For a full five seconds, he ran through every possible script for this-is-not-my-circus, but found none he could say.

"I'd appreciate it if I could see your delivery log for that day. The hand-delivered items."

"I'm afraid that's not possible—" he started, but the round of apologies were getting old. "For guest privacy reasons, we can't disclose—"

Geez, could you just cooperate a little? I pulled the zipper pouch from my shoulder bag and fished out the note in question. I slid it out of the envelope and across his desk, pointing out the single block-lettered words "Ms. Lily Davenport," in the careful hand of someone who'd seemed intent on staying anonymous.

"This isn't a fan letter," I said. "It's the fifth in a string of untraceable notes. If I have to involve law enforcement, I can do that."

Eric's professionalism held, but barely. He gave the note a hard stare, then checked my eyes for signs of a bluff. There were none. "I'll see what I can do," he said.

I thanked him, returned the envelope to its protective bag, and kept my seat while he vanished into another room. I zeroed in on an old-school message whiteboard on the wall to my left, half-erased with ghost handwriting that faintly showed. The board had a line about VIP ARRIVAL at 10:30, the last three digits hastily scrubbed. Other lines contained notes about client preferences, food allergies, and which rooms were to receive flower deliveries or champagne. I clocked a sticky note on the bottom edge: CHECK ROOM 304 KEY—RECURRING ISSUE.

Five minutes passed before Welles returned, harried, a ledger in his hands. He laid it on the desk, flipped to the page for the day in question, and angled it discreetly toward me. "You'll understand, of course, that I cannot let you make copies," he said.

I nodded. "Of course."

The log was written in black pen, each entry timed to the minute and initialed by the staffer on shift. I scanned the columns—Date, Recipient, Delivered By, Method,

Notes. There it was:

10:14 a.m., Ms. Davenport, delivered by Timothy B, method Hand, notes "Envelope found on concierge desk in lobby, requested room delivery, no sender info."

I pointed to the line. "Timothy B. is—?"

"A junior staffer. Bell service. He's not on the desk right now, but I can locate him for you."

"Please," I said.

He reached for his desk phone, pressed two digits, and spoke in a low tone. When he hung up, he informed me, "He will meet you at the bell captain's desk. Five minutes or so?"

That was my cue to leave his office.

While I waited, I did a slow lap of the lobby's perimeter, paying close attention to the staff hovering near the desk and the maintenance guy fiddling with a working light fixture. There was an undercurrent in the place— an invisible ripple. I saw it in the way the housekeeping supervisor checked her watch twice in one minute, and in the way two staffers at the espresso bar exchanged a rapid-fire sequence of glances at the main entrance.

Something had spooked the system. The notes, the Davenport name, or my inquiries? No matter. I was here to get answers.

I spotted Tim B. as he approached the bell captain's desk, looking around for the visitor who'd summoned him. He was a red-haired college kid, maybe twenty, with the start of a mustache on his upper lip. I stepped forward and introduced myself.

"My supervisor said you have some questions regarding a delivery for Ms. Davenport?"

"That's right. Is there somewhere we can talk privately?"

Tim licked his lips and gave a nervous nod toward the elevators. "Yeah, of course. Anything I can do, ma'am."

Ma'am. Yowch. Was I really giving off that much older of a vibe?

We bypassed the bank of elevators, traversed a short stretch of hallway, and Tim applied his employee badge to a card reader beside an unmarked door. The service corridor behind the Windsor's lobby presented an abrupt about-face. Gone was the vanilla-and-leather spa haze; here, the air was thick with ammonia, ancient coffee, and the existential damp of old plumbing. Exposed pipes ran overhead, and the linoleum underfoot gave a soft squeak with every step.

Tim led the way, three steps down the corridor, into a dead zone between the break room and the staff lockers. When he turned to face me, I could see the worry in his eyes.

"This isn't disciplinary," I said, keeping my voice low and pulling the stalker's envelope and my own small notebook from my bag. "I need you to walk me through what happened when you delivered this note to Ms. Davenport. From the top."

He fixed his eyes on a stain near my shoe. "Okay. Um, so—that morning, I was returning from making a delivery, and there was this lady in the lobby. She waved me over and handed me the envelope. She asked if I could take it straight up. Said it was time-sensitive."

"Did you recognize her?" I asked.

He shook his head. "Never seen her before. I assumed she was not a guest here."

"Describe her," I said. "Age, build, clothes, anything."

He squinted. "Uh, she was ... average? Mid-forties?

Not tall, not short … I'd say—regular. She had sunglasses, big ones, and a big purse or tote bag. Hat with a wide brim."

"Skin color?"

"Light. Not pale, but not tan."

"Accent?"

"I wasn't really paying attention to that, and she barely talked."

I digested that. "Anything else stand out?"

Tim's ears flushed, and he looked over his shoulder. "She tipped me. Fifty. Just for an envelope."

"That's generous," I said. "Was the envelope sealed?"

He nodded. "Yeah. Thick, too. Like extra-heavy paper, or like it had something else in it."

"Did you see her leave?"

He shook his head. "No. I went upstairs right away, handed off the envelope, and went straight to the bell desk. She was gone by that time."

"What was she wearing?"

He thought. "A dress, I think. Dark blue. And a long coat. Gloves, too, which was weird because it's, like, not that cold out."

"Gloves?" I said.

He nodded. "Yeah. Kind of dressy blue ones, like the color of the coat."

"Are you sure?"

"I mean—yeah, pretty sure. She kept her hands in her pockets mostly, but I saw them when she handed me the envelope and the money."

I noted this. "What about security cameras? The lobby's covered, right?"

"Um, yeah, I'm pretty sure. They're hidden pretty well."

"Was there anything else about the woman? Perfume,

jewelry, scar, limp—anything?"

He shook his head. "Sorry."

I grinned at him. "So, if she'd been twenty years younger and really pretty …"

He nodded, sheepish.

"You did fine, Tim. Thanks." I closed the notepad. "One other thing … I get that the hotel wants to protect its guests. But if someone is leaving threats—or tracking a public figure through your hotel—you need to take it seriously. If you see anything else, I'd like for you to get the manager involved."

A faint whiff of burnt toast came from the break room and the distant roar of a vacuum down the hall. I tucked the envelope into my bag and pulled out one of my cards.

"And if you remember anything else—anything at all—call me." I handed him the card, my phone number written in Sharpie on the back.

He took it with a nod. "I'll be in touch."

On my way out, I stopped and tapped on Adam Welles' door. He looked up, not thrilled to see me, I could tell.

"I got a decent description of what the suspect was wearing, but I'd like to check out your security footage. Maybe we'd catch a glimpse of her face on camera? If nothing else, it would be helpful for me to see how she moves, her stride, posture and such."

He glanced at the glass office, then at the hallway beyond it. "Ms. Parker, I must reiterate—hotel policy restricts surveillance review to—"

I put on my rueful face. "Perhaps it's better if we get the police involved. I've got a contact at home who could put in the request for an official investigation…"

The last thing any posh hotel wants is to have the

police poking around. "Right this way," he said with a sigh.

The security hub was down a flight of service stairs and through a door labeled AUTHORIZED PERSONNEL ONLY. Inside, the temperature dropped ten degrees; the room was windowless and lined with battered metal racks, every shelf cluttered with wires, surge protectors, and about five generations of routers. The wall opposite the door was dominated by three massive monitors, their glow the only real light in the space.

A heavyset man in a polo bearing the Windsor logo sat in a creaking office chair, a sandwich wrapped in a napkin in one hand and a remote in the other. "We got a guest issue?" he asked, scanning Welles, before fixing his gaze on me.

"Joseph, this is Ms. Parker," Adam said. "She's assisting with a guest security concern."

The guard nodded. "What's the situation?"

I filled him in.

He set down the sandwich, wiped his hands on his pants, and spun to the controls. "Lobby's got three cams, plus the main entrance. Give me a minute to find the right day and hour…" He navigated with the ease of someone who'd spent more of his life watching screens than making eye contact.

We watched as the time-stamped video rolled by. The lobby looked artificial on camera: guests floated through, bellhops zipped in and out, and Eric's analog image behind the desk checked in a woman in a pink tracksuit.

"Back it up," I said, when a blur of navy blue crossed the screen. "There. Pause. Slow-mo."

Joseph obliged, running the footage at quarter-speed. The woman in the hat and sunglasses entered from the rear elevator, a large tote slung over her left arm. She moved with a clipped, businesslike stride, but never faced the camera. Her approach to the concierge desk was from the side; she scanned the lobby while keeping her face hidden. I watched her wait near a planter of faux artichokes until Tim the bellhop stepped up to his post. She flagged him over, turned her head to shield her profile from the lens, and pressed the envelope into his hand.

"She's done this before," I said.

Joseph grunted. "Yeah, not her first rodeo. See how she waits until the desk's got at least two guests in line? No eyes on her, everyone's interacting with someone else."

"Can you run the entryway footage for the next five minutes?" I asked.

He clicked, and the view shifted. The woman emerged thirty seconds after she'd handed over the envelope, with both hands in her coat pockets, and exited through the covered drive-up without ever exposing her face.

"Is she a registered guest?" I asked.

Welles consulted a printed list. "There were no check-ins that appear to match. We had a guest in 417 who checked out this morning, but that was a male, solo."

"Could she have had an accomplice?" I asked.

He shrugged. "I have no idea, and there's nothing in the system for her. Unless she ghosted in on someone else's reservation."

I thought of the brown-haired man at the book signing, wondering if he could be the solo male guest. I wrote everything down, and flipped to a fresh page. "What about payment? Any cash rooms?"

Behind me, Welles practically snorted. "This is the Windsor. Everything's credit or direct bill. Nobody pays cash, unless it's for some special favor, maybe." He shifted on his feet. "There are sometimes comped rooms for VIPs or celebrity events, occasionally an emergency of some sort."

Joseph posed a question. "Could she have been booked through the event manager?"

"Possibly," Welles said. "But still, no one matches her on the sign-in logs."

I leaned in, scanning the screens for a better look at her gait, her posture, the little tics that speak volumes if you're paying attention. She walked with the intent of a person who'd memorized not only the route, but the exact timing of the cameras.

"She seems to know your system," I said to Joseph. "Has anyone else asked about your security setup in the last few weeks?"

He frowned, a tiny flicker of recognition. "Had a lady ask me for directions to the staff lounge two days ago. Said she was with corporate. Gave me a name, but I didn't check her badge and I really don't recall it."

I jotted it down. "She could have cased the whole place."

He nodded, his lips tight. "I'll monitor it. And I'll check the days before and after the one we watched. If she's pretending to be a guest here, she'll show up more than once."

I didn't hold much hope for that. Most likely, she'd learned where Lily was staying, studied the entrances and exits, and was only here long enough to drop off the note. If she was smart, she wouldn't want to be repeatedly caught on camera.

I turned to leave, but something near the door caught my

eye: a maintenance calendar tacked to the corkboard. The week's schedule was annotated with blocks of CAMERA OUTAGE—ROUTINE REBOOT at odd hours.

I pointed. "Who does the maintenance?"

"Contractor," Joseph said. "Outsourced to VisionTek. We don't handle the hardware ourselves."

I took a picture of the calendar and thanked Joseph for his help. In the hallway, Welles asked, "You think it's an inside job?"

"She may very well have help," I said. I didn't voice my worry that another envelope could arrive before Lily left the country. It wouldn't be unusual for a stalker to raise the stakes and increase the pressure.

I left the Windsor through the service exit, the city's noise smacking me. I felt the adrenaline letdown in my shoulders, but my mind was sprinting ahead. Whoever this woman was, she wasn't merely some disgruntled reader. She was a planner, a stalker with the time and resources—who could afford to chase someone around the world?—to make her point in a language only Lily would understand.

I texted Louisa to see if she was up for lunch. Something about chasing a suspect makes me hungry.

Chapter 10

Louisa was halfway across the city, having used her Opal card to take the train to one of the suburbs and enjoy a walk in Sydney Park, so I opted for a burger from a small local place so I could get on to my next stop. While I ate, I did a quick online search for the bookshop called Finch & Fig, a smaller store where Lily had done an afternoon signing the day before I met her and learned of her dilemma. I saw that it had the reputation of being the go-to for literary heavyweights and local academics, which meant you couldn't swing a tote bag without hitting a PhD.

From the outside, Finch & Fig looked like it had been airlifted from some Oxford alleyway and dropped, perfectly intact, into the Sydney business district. Leaded glass windows, door painted a proper British racing green, the sort of establishment where the neighborhood graffiti outside was spelled correctly. The bell above the door gave a reserved jingle as I stepped inside.

The interior was brighter than I would have expected, the high ceilings letting in gauzy sunlight through wavy glass. Polished wooden shelves lined every wall, with shelves, rolling ladders, and waist-high displays forming a sort of bookish labyrinth through the center. The air was a pleasing cocktail of ink, lemon-oil polish, and whatever pastry the staff had warmed up that morning.

I walked a slow circuit of the store, eyes on the details—exit routes, blind spots, places where a shy fan or a determined stalker might linger. The event display still dominated the front of the shop: a stack of *The Fifth Journey*, each copy fronted with a "Signed by Author!" sticker, flanked by two life-sized cardboard cutouts of Lily, one smiling, one serious.

Behind the main counter, a man with wire-rimmed glasses and the sort of orderly beard that suggested daily upkeep was organizing receipts into a ledger. He wore a dark button-down and a lanyard with three keys, each larger than the last. As I approached, he glanced up and assessed me with a retail poker face.

"Can I help you find something?" he asked, the accent pure local but softened by years of listening to an international clientele at close range.

I gave him my most non-threatening smile. "Just browsing, thanks. Actually, I missed the event here the other day—Lily Davenport's reading."

The expression flickered. "Ah, yes. Quite the turnout. We have a few signed copies left, if you're interested."

I shook my head. "Got one." Then, after a pause, "I'm actually a friend of Lily's. She asked me to check in about a small ... situation. Nothing to worry about, but someone's been following her tour a bit too closely for the usual superfan."

He set down the receipts, recalibrating his smile to polite-but-guarded. "We take our author events seriously here. Security, privacy, all that. Is there a problem?"

"Not a problem, exactly," I said, letting my voice drop into the calm assurance I used with nervous clients. "Only … well, something a bit off. Did you notice anyone at the event who seemed unusual? Someone hanging around before or after, watching Lily more intently than the average reader?"

He didn't answer right away, instead eyeing the security monitor behind the counter. The setup was an old-school four-way split, black and white, with feeds covering the register, front entrance, and two corners of the store I hadn't spotted yet.

"Our customers are literary types," he said, finally. "Not exactly the crowd for trouble. But with big events, you do get your share of odd ducks."

"Of course," I said, keeping it light. "But nothing that set off alarms this time?"

He gave a little huff of air, as if dismissing the idea, but I saw his fingers trace the keys on his lanyard. "The only thing out of the ordinary was how quickly Lily moved through the signing. She seemed anxious. Oftentimes, the authors hang around, chat up the staff, and pose for pictures. She was in and out in under ninety minutes, even with the crowd."

"She's been getting odd mail," I offered, "and I think it's starting to wear her down." I let that hang for a second, watching for his reaction. "Have you seen anyone hanging around the shop in the last week, asking about Lily's schedule, or when she'd be back?"

He shook his head. "No one asked about her after the event, and I haven't seen anyone lurking. Our regulars come and go like clockwork, and any new faces usually stand out. But..." He trailed off, uncertain.

"But?" I prompted.

He leaned in. "I recall a woman, now that you mention it. Not at the event, but the next morning. She came in right as we opened, said she'd left her bag behind during the reading. I let her look around, but she didn't find anything. Stayed a bit too long for nothing but a missing purse. I figured she was casing the shelves for a return trip, but ...?"

"Can you describe her?"

He pursed his lips, searching his memory. "Late forties, early fifties. Brown hair, streak of gray at the temples, very direct. British, or at least sounded it. She wore a long navy coat and carried a leather notebook."

The description piqued my interest. "Did you catch her name?"

He shook his head. "She didn't say, and I didn't ask. She wasn't rude, perhaps ... preoccupied. When she left, she walked straight down the block, didn't look back."

"She didn't leave her name in case you found her missing bag later?"

He shook his head.

"Did she buy anything?"

"No. She only wandered. Touched the display of autographed books a lot. You know how some people can't help picking up the merchandise, although they're not buying?"

I nodded. "Any chance your cameras caught her?"

He eyed the monitor. "Not unless she came to the register, which she didn't. The other feeds record over every day."

A dead end, but not a total loss. I pushed on. "What about during the event itself? Anyone who attended but didn't get a book signed, or who hung back and left without making a scene—the woman who came back, maybe?"

He considered. "I actually don't recall her from that previous afternoon. As for the others, there will be those who don't purchase anything. I recall a group of university students, but they all waited for selfies. A man in a suit, but he's a known reviewer for the *Herald*. Otherwise, the crowd was mostly women, book club types, very polite."

I thanked him for his time, took another slow walk around the store, eyes open for anything that might provide a clue. The space was immaculate, each shelf alphabetized and dusted, every display precisely arranged.

Before I left, the manager offered me a complimentary coffee. I accepted, if only to stall for another minute while I replayed the conversation in my head, wondering if he'd remembered something else.

As I sipped, he said, "If you think there's a real threat, we can beef up security for future events. I know a gent who does freelance detail—ex-military, very discreet."

"I'll let you know what I learn," I said, setting the cup down. "But for now, if that woman returns, try to get her name, or if you see anyone else who asks a bit too closely about Lily Davenport, call me." I handed him one of my RJP Investigations cards.

He studied it. "You really think it's that serious?"

"I think it's better to be careful," I said. "Literary types can be the most creative when it comes to making trouble."

He smiled at that, the tension easing from his jaw. "True. Well, I'll keep your card handy."

When his phone rang, I thanked him and made my way toward the door, pausing at the display one last time. The cardboard Lily stared back, her smile a shade too wide for the context.

Through the front windows I could see that the city was in full motion, the sidewalk alive with the shuffle of the lunchtime rush and the occasional jogger. I perched on one of their wingback chairs, jotting down what I'd learned, which helped fill in the gaps in what I'd learned earlier at the hotel: a woman with a British accent, brown hair, long navy coat, her presence at the store following the event.

It wasn't much, but a lead, nevertheless. And it could be all I needed to get the next piece of the puzzle.

My coffee was gone, and I tossed the cup in a recycle bin near the desk, debating my next move. The woman's behavior didn't match many classic stalker patterns—no gifts, no direct approach, no escalation. She didn't seem to be enticing Lily to come toward her. She watched, she waited, she studied. If she was the sole one behind the notes, she was playing the long game.

I should check nearby hotels, see if I could learn her identity, but without a photo of the woman's face, I doubted I would get anywhere. I was halfway to the door, rehearsing the description in my head, when a voice piped up from behind a freestanding display of Bestsellers of the Decade.

"Excuse me," a female voice said, "but did you say you're looking for someone who's a fan of Lily Davenport?"

The speaker emerged from behind the stack. She

couldn't have been older than twenty-five, with short auburn hair and a thrift-store blazer that was either a bold fashion choice or the result of a very hasty morning. Her arms were full of paperbacks, and she set them down with a gentle thump.

The manager looked over, momentarily surprised. "Hazel, do you have something?"

Hazel gave a quick, nervous smile, then looked at me. "Sorry, I wasn't eavesdropping, but I think I know who you're talking about. I did the line management at the event, so I saw everyone up close. There was this woman—she came in late, didn't buy a book, but hung around during the Q&A. She looked as if she was memorizing everything. Not in a creepy way. I'd say … very focused. Okay, yeah, maybe a little creepy."

I pulled out my notepad. "Do you remember what she looked like?"

Hazel nodded, tilting her head as she recalled the image. "Older than most of the crowd, but not ancient. Late fifties? Her hair was brown, but with these gray stripes at the temples—but chic, you know? She wore a suit, very buttoned-up, and these old-fashioned lace-up shoes."

"Did she interact with Lily at all?" I asked.

Hazel hesitated. "Not directly. She didn't come up for a signature. I asked, because I was trying to make sure everyone got their book signed if they wanted. She said, 'No, thank you, I prefer to observe.' But she didn't take her eyes off Lily the whole time."

The manager, now interested, interjected. "Was this the same woman who came in the next morning about the lost bag?"

"I don't recall that one. Must have been before I got

to work that day. I remember this one because she asked me where Lily was going next. She knew about the Rome event—said it before I could look it up. She knew the whole itinerary by heart."

I scribbled, suit, lace-ups, touches of gray. "Did she give you a name?"

Hazel frowned, thinking. "She said it at one point, but I'm blanking. Something with an A? Anna? Amanda?"

I felt a ping of excitement. "Did she have an accent?"

"Yeah, definitely British," Hazel said. "She talked like someone who's taught at university forever. Really precise."

"Did you notice anything else about her? Any nervous habits, or the way she moved?"

Hazel brightened. "Yes, actually. She kept pulling out this fancy notebook and writing in it. Like, constantly. It wasn't a regular Moleskine, either—it was super expensive, real leather. She wrote during the reading. I thought she might be a journalist, but she didn't take photos or anything."

"Did she talk to anyone else?" I asked.

Hazel shrugged. "Not that I saw. She watched, wrote things down, and left when everyone else started crowding Lily for photos. Almost like she wanted to be invisible."

The manager, who had been listening with a faint air of disappointment, looked slightly impressed. "You have a good memory for detail," he said.

Hazel flushed. "I've worked six of these signings in the last two months. You learn to spot the outliers."

I flipped to a fresh page. "Did she mention where she was staying, or anything about herself?"

"No. She seemed really private. But she definitely knew the author's schedule better than I did."

I tucked the notebook away, then gave her my card. "If she comes back, or if you remember anything else, can you call me?"

She looked at my card as if it were a lottery ticket. "A private investigator! Definitely. I actually hope she does come back—she was kind of fascinating."

I thanked her and turned to the manager. "You've got a good team," I said, and meant it.

He gave Hazel a look that was half-appraisal, half-surprise, as if seeing her in a new light. "She's our best," he said, and Hazel blushed again.

As I left, I tried to imagine the woman—Amanda or Anna, or something else entirely—standing at the back of the event, watching Lily with that predatory calm. It was a detail many wouldn't notice.

I crossed the street, found a bench, and sat with my notes. Graying brown hair. British accent. Knows the itinerary. Expensive notebook. "Intense but private." I wrote the phrase in all caps and circled it twice. For now, it moved the male suspect quite a bit lower on my list.

I considered the notes themselves. Every one had been elegant, left-tilting script, with a flourish to the 'A' at the end. It wasn't a coincidence that the bookseller had picked up on the notebook, or that the woman seemed less interested in the author's book than in the process of watching the celebrity at work. This was someone who was there for a purpose.

I imagined the woman sitting with a notebook on her lap, writing as Lily spoke. She could have been recording the reading verbatim, or she was writing her own version, or maybe she was composing the next cryptic note as she watched. She didn't need to approach Lily in person; the point was to let the author feel the pressure from a distance.

A tactic that was almost poetic. Almost.

And if she was following the tour, she'd be at the next event, or the hotel, or somewhere else within Lily's orbit.

I texted Louisa: Hazel at Finch & Fig ID'd our A. British, mid-50s, gray at temples, expensive notebook. Possible name Anna or Amanda. Check event guest list?

Louisa replied instantly: Will do. Tell Hazel she's a star.

I smiled, then phoned the Windsor to see if Joseph in the security room had spotted our suspect at any other times on the video feed.

A long shot, but why not?

Chapter 11

The next morning, we found Lily in her suite. She wore loose gray pants and a sloppy blue cardigan, and her hair hung limp and shapeless. She let us inside and slumped into an armchair, her posture folded in on itself, arms wrapped around her ribs. The notes were spread on the side table, fanned out and slightly curled from her fidgeting with them. Louisa immediately offered to make tea.

"Rough night?" I asked, setting my laptop bag beside the sofa.

"A man approached me on the street, a thin creature wearing a long, dark coat. I'd only popped out for a packet of biscuits. I've found the most delicious ones here, almond flavor—never mind that. It didn't seem worth asking my local escort person to come when I only meant to walk two blocks to the shop and back."

"This man?"

"Yes, well, in retrospect, I think he was simply someone a bit down on his luck who hoped I'd have a few dollars. But I honestly don't know. He startled me so badly I shrieked. When a passing couple paused to see if I was all right, he'd disappeared round a corner or something."

"Did he say anything? Anything at all?" Louisa asked.

Lily shook her head, giving me a sideways glance, face pale, eyes clear but underscored with dark smudges. "At any rate, I barely slept. Every time I closed my eyes, I kept either seeing the man in the dark coat or obsessing about these notes, over and over. There's something about the actual paper. The way it smells. I can't recall what it's from, but it's—" She stood and made a vague gesture, like flicking lint from a shirt.

"Give it time," I said, figuring I'd learned all I was going to about the man who'd approached her. I turned back to the notes and asked Lily to hold each one in sequence, and as she did, I watched for micro-expressions.

"You react strongest to this one," I said, pointing to the Sydney letter.

She nodded. "I suppose because it's the most recent. Five contacts now, not to mention being approached by that man last night—it's the straw that's breaking the camel's back." She turned away and paced the strip of carpet between the fireplace and the window, hands buried in her cardigan pockets.

From the coffee bar in the corner, Louisa observed, "You're going to wear a hole in that carpet, love."

"Sorry," Lily said, but didn't stop moving.

Louisa turned toward us, carrying a lacquered tray with three mugs of tea. She set it on the coffee table, but gave me a look before picking up a cup for herself and retreating to her preferred post in the window seat.

"Let's try something else," I said, keeping my voice level. "Forget the notes for a minute. Tell me about your life within the past few years. Jobs, events, travels, or anything unusual."

Lily exhaled through her nose, leaning against the mantel, holding her teacup between her palms. "Well … five years ago, I'd recently finished my second book, waiting to see how the first one would do in sales. I'd been teaching for ten years or so, part-time, and I was living alone in Camden Borough. I traveled a bit, but nothing interesting—readings, conferences. I went briefly to Scotland for my mother's funeral, if that's of any importance."

"You mentioned that the paper itself seems to resonate with you. I'm angling for anything that could link you to it," I said, showing her the fifth note once more. "Think about your teaching … or workshops, writing groups, retreats. Places where you handled a lot of correspondence. Could you have used, or handled, this particular paper stock?"

Her lips moved, counting off memories. "There was the Bloomsbury residency, the summer at Arvon, and a short thing at Faber. But all of those used institutional letterhead. The only time I remember writing by hand was the London workshop series I ran for—" She stopped, then turned to face me. "That's odd. For a small group, in 2017. But we didn't have fancy stationery, did we?"

Louisa, who had been staring into her tea, set it down with a sudden, decisive clink. "Wait. That workshop. I attended it. Wasn't that the one where the program manager splurged on custom note paper? Someone commented that it made them feel like a banker."

Lily's face changed in an instant, the memory surfacing

like the shock of a cold wave. "Yes! They bought this absurdly nice paper, as you might see for a will. The whole point was to make the feedback feel substantial, permanent."

"Exactly," Louisa said, turning to me with a proud, nearly maternal grin. "Lily wrote feedback letters to every participant. In her own hand. Very ceremonial, impressive."

I took out my notebook, writing 'London, 2017, Workshop' in all caps and underlining it twice. "Describe the stationery."

"A5, heavy cream stock, and, yes, this exact tooth—the surface feel of it—not too slick, not too rough. And we used blue ink. The workshop sponsor—a fussy woman—insisted it was more personal…" Her voice trailed off, her eyes focusing on the five notes, as she began to see where this was going.

"Was it a large class?" I asked.

She ran her fingers through her hair, loose and wild from the long night. "No, perhaps ten people. Twelve, max. We were a closed group—everyone had to submit a sample and be approved. We met in a private room above a pub in Holborn. It ran for eight weeks."

"Yes!" Louisa chimed in. "Such a cozy and magical-feeling place."

"Do you remember the participants' names?" I asked, and when she hesitated, I pressed. "As many as you can. We can fill in the rest later."

Lily stared toward the ceiling, recalling as she listed names. "An Amanda—young American, very sharp. A guy named George, South African, wore a jacket even in July. Helen, she was Australian, actually. She had this incredibly silly laugh, like a goose honking. And there was—oh, what was her name? The shy one. Something … Morris, or Morrison. She barely spoke, but when she did, she came up with some killer lines."

She turned her attention to Louisa, eyebrows raised. "That's only five, including yourself. Help? Ideas?"

I wrote the names, underlining Amanda's, and let my pen rest on the page. Someone else had brought up that name in recent days.

Lily must have noticed. "You think it's her?"

"I don't know … an American, and younger than the others," I said, wondering if this Amanda might have faked her accent. "What else do you remember about any of them?"

Lily shrugged. "One woman was older than most of the group, I'd say late forties. She had a limp, but not always—you only saw it when she was tired. Her writing was quite decent. Really dark stuff, but with potential. The kind that makes you look over your shoulder after you read it."

Louisa piped up from the window. "Right, the shy one. She gave you a signed copy of her manuscript at the end, didn't she?"

Lily blinked, then nodded. "That's right, she did. But I never read the whole thing. There was something about having it—I don't know. I generally didn't hold onto anything my students produced. I believe I mailed it back to her."

I looked at the third note, and once again at my own scribbles. "Did you ever see this Amanda, after the workshop?"

"No," Lily said. "A couple of the participants sent thank you emails, including Helen from Melbourne and you, Louisa, but I don't recall if I actually replied. I was deeply into my own manuscript at the time."

Louisa snorted at a recollection. "Oh yes, Morris, I believe it was. You were scared of her, admit it."

Lily frowned. "She was intense, and the writing was quite dark."

I underlined *Amanda* three times. "If she's the one behind this, she'd have had access to your handwriting, the feedback letters, the stationery. Did the workshop sessions ever get contentious? Arguments, disagreements?"

"Not really," Lily said. "Although, truthfully, everyone *was* competing for approval. Amanda was vivacious and eager to learn, while the older lady was the quiet one, and the gentleman from South Africa seemed to crave praise."

I closed my notebook. "Do you still have the group email list? I can try to track them down, see where they are now."

Lily hesitated. "It was on my old laptop, but everything gets saved to the cloud these days. I can probably dig it up."

"Do that," I said. "And if you remember anything else about Amanda—or about anyone else from the workshop—let me know."

Lily's posture loosened a notch. "Thank you," she said, voice steadier. "I feel better having a few names. At least the stationery is a direction."

Louisa slid off the window seat and crossed the room, picking up the teapot and pouring tea. "You're both overthinking it," she said. "It's clearly her. The only question is why she waited so long to start this harassment."

Too many of the details didn't fit—the age of the American woman, the graying hair, the British accent Hazel had mentioned. I doubted Louisa was right, but I watched Lily for her reaction. She only sipped her tea and stared into the middle distance, lips pursed in thought.

"Jealousy, perhaps," she said at last. "Or a sense of drama."

"We shall figure this out, and we'll get her," I said, more for myself than for them.

I almost believed it.

Chapter 12

After the conversation with Lily, I found myself thinking about the notepaper itself rather than the content of the messages. I'm as big a fan of fancy stationery as anyone, which is to say it's not often tops on my mind, and the finer points are way outside my wheelhouse. I needed an expert.

A quick search on my phone showed the address of 'Sydney's Premier Stationer' and a tap on the map showed the location to be a couple of train stops away. Louisa had convinced Lily that the two of them should leave the hotel, incognito, and take the ferry to Manly Beach for an afternoon of touristy shopping. So, I was on my own.

I navigated the trains like a pro, considering my very limited experience on public transportation, and soon found myself entering a tiny shop, crammed between a dumpling restaurant and a lighting store, on King Street.

As I entered the tiny shop that gave off the heady smell of fine paper, the only person in sight was an elderly man in brown pants, a pale tan shirt, and a vest. He looked up at me over the top of his wire-framed reading glasses.

"Hi, I wonder if you might help me identify a brand of stationery by looking at one sheet of it?"

"I'll do my best." Confident, but not a braggart. I liked that. "Martin Tantingham, at your service."

On my way over, I'd concocted a background story about how my grandmother loved to write letters on quality paper. I'd come across this sheet and hoped to get a box of it for her. With his focus entirely on the paper itself, rather than the content of the message, Martin held the sheet to the light from the shop's front window. His fingers gently caressed the surface.

"It's very good paper," he said. "First, the tactile: the stock is heavy, somewhere north of 120 GSM—that's grams per square meter—perhaps 140. Not the sort of thing you find in a hotel business center or discount store. There's a softness to the surface, a nap, which can mean the sheet was pressed by hand rather than machine."

"You can tell all that by touching it? I'm impressed."

He picked up a ruler and measured the note. "It's 14.8 mm by 21.0 mm, dead on A5. And the envelope is an identical match, seems to have been glued with a broad, flat brush and it was pried very carefully open so as not to rip it." He held the page to his nose. "A faint scent of lavender, not from the paper, but likely from the sender's hands or storage."

I filed all this away mentally, not quite sure how relevant it would be but fascinated by the details Martin was picking up.

"Now, the color—cream, but not the commercial vanilla you would commonly find."

I could see what he meant. This was a shade richer, a half-step toward old book pages, the sort of hue that makes you think of libraries and legal documents.

"The handwriting, do you think the ink is a special type?"

"Definitely done by a top-quality pen and high-end ink." He handed the note to me. "As to where you would find such a thing, I regret to say it's not here at my shop. The paper is from the Regency Collection in London."

He looked up and gave an almost imperceptible wink. "I recognized it from the watermark. I carried a few boxes of it, at least a decade ago, but it proved a bit too rich for my clientele. Took me years to sell what I had, and I decided not to reorder."

"London, hm? Any idea what shops would carry this Regency paper?"

"Might try Pembroke's in Notting Hill. Give the information we've discussed and perhaps they can locate it for you."

I thanked him profusely and ended up buying a beautiful fountain pen that would have normally been way beyond my budget because he'd been so helpful. Or maybe because of the subtle wink.

With Lily's note and my new fountain pen in my bag, I set out and decided to stroll King Street in search of some lunch. A group of intricate glass light fixtures in the window of a Turkish restaurant caught my eye. Why not?

While I waited for my bowl of lamb stew, I wrote out a bulleted list of Martin Tantingham's comments in my notebook, adding my own observations about the style of the writer:

—Pembroke's, Notting Hill (why is this familiar sounding?)

—Paper: A5, cream, heavy, handmade

—Regency watermark

—Envelope: matched stock, sealed with brush

—Ink: blue, fountain pen, pools at line start

—Handwriting: left-leaning, joined, precise

—Smell: faint lavender

And since the restaurant was crowded, and the service was taking a few minutes, I performed a quick search on my phone. There it was—Pembroke's Stationery, a Notting Hill institution. I clicked through and recognized the branding—midnight blue and gold logo, and a photo of the storefront. I'd been to this place, a side trip for another client once on my way to visit Louisa in Bury. The store manager, Ellen, had been most helpful and reassured me I could contact her any time. I scanned the catalog, filtering for A5, then for cream, then for artisanal or hand-pressed.

There it was: The Regency Collection, described as "painstakingly crafted in small batches using traditional rag methods." The price per twenty sheets was obscene, and the envelope bundles cost even more. I saved the product photo and compared it to the note. The match was nearly perfect.

I wondered if the store kept a customer log—some of the boutique shops did, for VIPs or repeat buyers.

But when my savory stew arrived, along with some wonderful, garlicky bread pieces, I forgot all about stationery and ink for a while.

Chapter 13

I closed my laptop when Louisa walked into our suite. "How was your afternoon?"

"Lovely. I'd say perfect. Getting out in the fresh air, being on the water ... Lily relaxed for the first time since we've been here. I've been quite concerned for her mental state, and I could tell it was good for her, having a day without worry. We ended with a lovely dinner in the restaurant at her hotel." She leaned over and gave me a peck on the cheek. "And how was yours?"

I filled her in on the details of my visit to the local stationery shop. "It seems like a good lead on where the stalker probably purchased the paper for the notes. It's fairly expensive stuff and not widely available. I located the outlet in London—well, Notting Hill—and I'm waiting for a response to my email inquiry."

"I could use a bedtime cup of tea and am most ready to get out of these shoes," she said, heading for her bedroom.

My phone chimed with an incoming email and my pulse picked up when I saw it was from Ellen at Pembroke's. *If it's not too late in Sydney, I'll call you with some information,* she'd written. *Fifteen or twenty minutes? As soon as my current customer is finished.*

I quickly shot off an answer that anytime in the next hour would be fine.

While waiting, I poked around the internet for writing workshops in England and found the London workshop's Facebook page. I went through all the posts, scanning the faces and names, deciding it was a lost cause since the workshops led by Lily had taken place over five years ago.

At 10:41 p.m., my phone rang. It was Ellen's voice. "Charlie! I love that you remember I am the Stationery Oracle."

We exchanged a few pleasantries but soon got right to the point.

"Short answer: Yes, that paper is ours. Only three customers have bought more than ten sheets of Regency A5 in the last six months. One is an estate lawyer, one is a retired general who writes love letters to his French mistress (don't ask), and the third … yes, this is strange … a woman paid cash, said it was for 'personal correspondence,' and declined to be added to the customer registry. She bought 20 sheets, 10 envelopes. This was about five weeks ago. Are you on another mysterious case?"

I gave her the quick rundown: the client, the threats, the need to know about the third customer.

Ellen was delighted, although she apologized for not knowing greater details. "You get all sorts at Pembroke's, but this one stood out. She had an air of academia, mid-fifties, wore a navy coat and the largest sunglasses I've ever seen. She wore gloves, which I only noticed as odd because she handled the paper without ever actually touching it. Most customers can't wait to caress the stock. She was almost clinical. She paid in cash, exact change, and declined all help choosing the paper. Very sure of herself."

I asked about the accent.

"British, but not London. I'm guessing northern? Or private school. She didn't linger—just bought, counted the envelopes, and left."

"Any name?"

"None given. I would check our CCTV, but the system refreshes every month. Sorry, love."

I thanked her, promised to send her a signed copy of Lily's book, and hung up. I added the new details to my notes. In addition to the navy coat and sunglasses, we'd learned she paid cash, had an academic air, and the purchase date of the stationery was five weeks ago.

The timeline fit. The first note to Lily had appeared three weeks ago, in London, slipped under the door of her hotel room. This woman—our 'A'—had bought the materials locally, with at least a two-week lead time. That level of preparation screamed either obsessive planning or a talent for escalation. I wondered which was more dangerous.

I started an email to Lily: Breakthrough—paper traced to Pembroke's, Notting Hill. A woman purchased this paper in person, cash, 20 sheets/10 envelopes. Description matches the sightings on camera here in Sydney. Will update in person. CP.

After the email whooshed away, I slid the note back

into its envelope and ran my thumb along the seam. I thought about how far it had traveled: from London, to the hotel, to Lily, to me. How each handoff was invisible, but each left a trace.

Feeling inspired, I wrote in my notebook, below the bulleted list: People who use fine stationery believe in the weight of the written word; people who buy it in cash, leave no name, and plan weeks ahead believe in something else—but what?

I set the lamp to low and tidied my desk, leaving only the single note in its envelope at the center. I wondered if the sender of the notes had felt the same small, obsessive satisfaction as I did now. I doubted it. The feeling wasn't pride. It was closer to relief.

Through Louisa's open bedroom door, I saw her snuggled within the covers of her bed, sound asleep. Poor thing. I knew she was worried about her friend. Obviously, sleep was the bigger lure than a cup of evening tea. I switched off her light and shut the door gently.

As I closed my laptop and checked the lock on the suite's door, I felt the satisfaction of a day with some solid answers. And yet, there were questions. When would the stalker reach out the next time?

It was nearly midnight. Sydney outside was muffled, rain beginning to streak the windows. I didn't bother with the curtains; I wanted to wake to the sight of the city.

Chapter 14

The woman tossed her wide-brimmed hat aside and sat at the table in her room. She slid a sheet of the special paper toward her, a little nervous because she had only two sheets left; she dared not make a mistake and spoil it. She'd been considering the exact wording for days as she stood in the shadows and watched the other hotel. Even when she boarded the ferry this afternoon for Manly Beach, quite a spur-of-the-moment decision.

Would the *great* Lily Davenport have remembered her, dressed so differently today in bright colors? Twice, she'd had to abruptly turn her back when she realized with a shock that the older woman with Lily was someone she'd met, someone from that workshop. But it was fascinating to watch the pair, to trail along behind as they laughed and ate ice cream, completely unaware of her presence.

She tapped her pen on the desktop. Should she add something to the note about that? About the fact she'd known the celebrity author's every move today, that she had actually watched her in every city along the tour, at times had been close enough to touch her, close enough to draw a weapon if she'd felt so inclined? What about adding the real reason she hated this woman so much — the betrayal she'd held in her heart all these years?

A flashback to the room over that pub, where she'd shared her most sacred words, where she'd poured out her heart on the page. A fictional story, yes, but one in which she'd bared her most intense feelings. Her words—now stolen.

An unbidden picture of Candy's reaction upon reading the manuscript hit her full force. What did her daughter know about what it meant to be a novelist anyway, when she rolled her eyes and said, "Well, Mum, it's a start, but I wouldn't send it off to a publisher."

The woman realized her entire hand ached from gripping her pen so tightly.

No. The wording of the note was something she'd carefully calculated from the beginning. She set the pen down, paced the length of the room twice, and shook the tremble out of her hands before picking it up. She wrote out the words and added her initial at the end with a flourish, then glanced at the clock on the bedstand as she sealed the envelope. 11:23 p.m. Time to move!

She slipped into her long coat, pocketed the letter, and picked up her wide-brimmed hat. She would blend in with the Windsor's late-evening crowd, returning to their rooms, and if the cameras spotted her, what of it? She was well covered and would not raise her eyes toward them.

Or maybe she would. She was beginning to feel increasingly daring by the minute.

Chapter 15

I woke before six to the sound of rain, light but persistent, rattling the tall windows and pooling in the stone troughs below. The note was where I'd left it, next to the lamp and a half-empty cup of water. I wished a solution had magically appeared overnight. No such luck, but no real surprise. I moved on to the coffee bar in the corner and started a cup brewing.

At 7:05, my phone, set to vibrate, danced a tiny jig across the tabletop. The screen lit with Lily's name.

"Good morning! I understand you and Louisa had a wonderful afternoon and evening. She's not awake yet, so it must have been good."

"Charlie, there's—" Her voice cracked.

"Oh no, what is it? Another note?" Somehow I had a feeling.

"Yes, it was pushed under the door to my room sometime during the night."

"I'll get dressed and come right over."

"There's no need. I phoned the security manager before I touched the envelope. He watched, as my witness, when I opened it and saw it was from the same person."

"They have security cameras, surely, in the hallways throughout the hotel?"

"Yes, and I went downstairs and viewed the footage with him. The figure in the video is the same one the witnesses described—the long, navy-blue coat and wide-brimmed hat. She—I'm fairly certain it's a woman—is shown entering through the lobby front door with a crowd of people, riding a separate elevator to my floor and walking directly to my door. Charlie, she knows where I'm sleeping." A sob escaped.

"I don't suppose there are any shots that reveal her face?"

"No. She was extremely careful. Slipped the note under my door and was on the way down the stairs at the end of the hall in less than thirty seconds. A minute later, a camera in the courtyard showed her passing the swimming pool. There's nothing after that."

"Have the hotel manager move you to another room right away."

"It's being arranged as we speak."

"It might be a good idea for you to switch hotels with us. I could stay in your room and you move in here with Louisa. You *are* in the city for a couple more days."

"It won't matter." Her voice sounded resigned. "Here's what the latest note says. It's only a single line. *'I shall have what I came for. Rome will be the last. A.'* And Charlie ... she's escalated the threat. There's a hand-drawn sketch of a dagger, right below the wording. I have no idea what she means by saying 'what I came for.' What on earth is that?"

I had no idea either, and it was making my head hurt. The inclusion of the sketch was definitely worrisome. It could mean the stalker was about to get physical.

"So, this ... whatever it is she wants ... it will happen in Rome?" Lily's voice was terse.

"Sounds like she wants it to end there. My guess is that she has a plan for the final message. Or for you, personally."

A long silence, followed by a shaky sigh. She cleared her throat. "I don't know what she wants, whether the threat is to my physical safety or my reputation. But I'll be ready."

I told her to call me immediately if she received any new messages, no matter how trivial they might seem, and to let me know if anyone approached her in person.

I had Lily re-read the note, wrote it down verbatim, thanked her, and disconnected. I sat back, fingers steepled, and ran through the call in my head. I didn't need to ask whether it was written on the same paper, in the same hand, with the same ink. I knew it was.

Whoever the stalker was, she was methodical, literate, precise, obsessed with the past, and committed to anonymity even as she seemed to demand acknowledgment. I wished we had a name. At least we could ask the local police to help with the search.

Louisa emerged from her room, brewed a cup of tea, and leaned against the desk's edge. "Are you going to tell Lily about the Pembroke's match?"

"Actually, there's a more pressing development."

Her face went pale as I repeated Lily's call and the contents of the newest note. "She's scared. She wants to see the end of this."

Louisa nodded with a memory. "She always did love a tricky conclusion. All of her books are written with a surprise twist at the end."

I let the idea hang in the air.

My phone vibrated. This time, I saw an unfamiliar number with a UK country code. I answered, thinking it could be Ellen from Notting Hill.

Dead silence, then the call dropped.

I looked at the notes on the desk, opened my laptop, and told Louisa, "We should plan on going to Rome."

She raised an eyebrow. "All roads, darling?"

I smiled at the reference, but began entering search criteria for changing our flights. I found an itinerary that would work, and placed a forty-eight-hour hold on two seats, on the same flight as Lily's. If we could catch the crazy stalker here in Sydney, we might not need to leave, but now we had a way to follow through. In case.

While I searched for tickets, Louisa had showered and dressed. "We should stay close to Lily today," she decided. "It's not good for her to be alone. Too much time to think."

True, the street fair event wasn't until tomorrow, and I didn't think any of us needed to be sitting around our hotel rooms, stewing. My brain whirled with details, trying to figure out how this stalker's mind worked. She must have known what it would look like from this end, how each step would lead us inevitably to the images on the cameras. It could be that was the point. To be seen and to be sure we couldn't identify her.

Outside, the rain had stopped. Through the glass, the city looked newly invented, shiny and clean.

"I'll call Lily and suggest breakfast somewhere quiet

and small." My aunt had her phone out and was scrolling her contacts.

What they lined up was definitely quiet, and nowhere near small. Lily informed Louisa that she'd been moved into the presidential suite at the Windsor and had ordered a room service breakfast. She would have the kitchen triple the order and hold it until we arrived.

It fit perfectly with my idea that we should make a plan to beef up security around both of Louisa's remaining Sydney events. I felt sure her publisher would help arrange for some discreet, but husky, private guards to mill about during the street fair tomorrow. And, no doubt, there would be a security presence at the publisher's private party the next night, as well. I would stress the idea that we wanted to keep Lily safe but also to catch this woman in the navy coat and stop the harassment. For good. And we had less than three days to end this before we'd have to leave the country.

Chapter 16

The hotel's cheap blackout curtains let through only the faintest cuticle of sodium light from the noisy street below, enough to make the room feel like a bunker rather than a haven for rest. Since delivering her latest missive to the Windsor, she'd felt the charge of adrenaline, the excitement of a mission drawing down to its final days. Her long coat and wide-brimmed hat lay on the undisturbed bed. The red glow of the bedside clock said it was after five a.m. but sleep eluded her.

She sat cross-legged on the thin blue carpet, surveying her literary empire of photocopied manuscripts, classroom notes, and battered notebooks.

Mum, why do you keep this old stuff? Writers write. Get on with something new.

"Shut up, Candace Lynne Morris. What do you know,

anyway? You file papers all day at the registry office. You know nothing of what it is to be a literary figure." She uttered the words aloud, although the conversation had taken place at least two years ago.

Mum, it's an obsession with you, keeping all this tattered old paper.

But Candy was wrong. She had method, not madness, or so she reminded herself as she arranged the papers into piles that only she would recognize as chronological: workshop feedback, literary magazine rejection slips, her own drafts, heavily notated and dog-eared from five years of revision. She worked in silence, the only sound the ritual rustle of paper and the soft, arrhythmic click of her tongue against the roof of her mouth.

Her battered workshop folder, the one with the spine held together by strips of floral washi tape, lived at the center of it all. She reached for it, hands precise and reverent, and pulled out a flagged page—one of the many marked with bright tabs. This was where it began: her story, her character, her voice.

She ran her finger down the margin, tracing the curlicue of her own written words, and the darker, angular commentary in another hand: Bold. Unexpected!

The exclamation point after *unexpected* had seemed faintly patronizing, like an afterthought from a teacher required to offer at least one positive per critique. She found herself mouthing the phrase as she read it, her lips barely moving, echoing words from the past.

She set the folder aside and plucked a hardcover from the adjacent stack. *The Fifth Journey*, first UK edition, dust jacket becoming slightly tattered from weeks in a suitcase. She opened it to the passage she had memorized months ago, the one that had triggered her to take action. She read it in the glow of the room's only working lamp, mouthing the sentences, flipping to her own draft to compare, to tally, to confirm.

The similarities were there—buried beneath layers of cosmetic difference, of course, but obvious in *her* mind. A phrase here, a fragment of description there, all rewritten in the other woman's so-called voice. The thievery was so deft it nearly deserved respect.

From a page of her folder, a picture fell out: a group photo from the last day of the London workshop. Lily Davenport, not yet famous, stood at the center of the small group, smiling for the camera, as were all the others. The other participants had scrawled messages on the back—all of them wannabe writers who hoped to be published one day. Some had achieved the goal, but none to the level of acclaim as Lily. She looked past Lily to the others in the shot: the expectant faces, the clinging hope, the fear of their own inferiority.

Picking up her ancient composition book, she jammed the photo between the pages and returned to the comparison. She had done this before—dozens of times over the years. With her blue fountain pen (the same shade as the ink in Lily's signed copies, she had noted), she circled and underlined the passages that reinforced her belief.

"My words," she whispered. She circled the phrase repeatedly, harder. The point of the pen tore the paper, leaving a blue welt in the cheap composition stock. "Not madness, Candy, I deserve justice." Rage flooded through her.

A noise sounded out in the corridor, another sleepless hotel guest, or perhaps someone checking out early.

She slid the notebook closer, her hands shaking, and re-read her original story. It was not perfect—she could admit that—but it was hers. The character, the plot twist, the final image of the protagonist standing alone in a rain-slicked city, searching for something she could not name. And there, on page 312 of *The Fifth Journey*, was the so-similar image of a rainy city, the same lonely girl. Yes, Lily's version was rendered in sleeker prose but unmistakably similar.

She closed her eyes and let the anger come—a wave of hot, cleansing rage that made her scalp prickle and her tongue go dry. In her imagination, she could smell the old workshop room: stale coffee, chalk dust, the faint chemical sweetness of ink. She could hear the way Lily offered advice on scene and character.

A lonely girl on a rainy street. Did the similarity end there? No—she would not believe it.

She opened her eyes and scrawled a note in the margin: "Will *not* go unpunished." Her handwriting grew sloppier, aggressive, the loops of her letters swelling. She underscored the words three times, then returned to the evidence pile.

On the desk sat a stack of printed emails—rejection letters from literary agents and editors. She sorted them, pulling out the one she normally read last: the rejection from the publisher who eventually bought Lily's book.

She read it aloud, voice gaining strength as she went. "Your submission shows promise, but could do with some editorial help and polishing. Unfortunately, the market is saturated with similar narratives at present."

She slammed the letter down and picked up Lily's hardcover, her eyes landing on the reviews. She read the blurbs aloud in a voice pitched for maximum irony. "'A narrative so fresh it borders on the unthinkable.' Yes, unthinkable, if you're the sort who can't remember what you've stolen." She snorted—a wet, bitter sound. Flipping to the back page, the author's photo smiled toward the world.

"Original? What a lie," she sneered, the word turning to bile. She stabbed the photo with the tip of her pen, blue ink blossoming across the famous author's glossy cheek.

As she stared, her breathing slowed, her vision tunneled to the neat lines of blue on white in her notebook. It was not about winning, she realized. This was about being seen, being acknowledged. The world had conspired to erase her, but she would not let it succeed.

The perfect Lily Davenport would get her just reward when her sterling reputation was ruined forever.

She capped the pen, stared at the ink-stained tips of her fingers, then at the pages spread before her. Two days, she thought. She would continue to watch, and she would deliver the message, the final note, the one that could not be ignored.

She closed her notebook and finally allowed herself to feel tired.

She would sleep. But when she woke, she would be ready.

Chapter 17

The Sydney street fair spanned the length of three city blocks, with a couple of wide spots where the festivity poured over onto vacant lots. The wide blue sky, temperature in the fifties, and fresh breeze off the harbor were welcome indeed after yesterday's steady rain.

The organizers had draped bunting across the intersections, paper pennants fluttering in the breeze. The crowd was a swarm of families, students, and vendors offering everything from art prints to kangaroo-printed pajamas, to candles and incense burners. Street food vendors shouted over one another, and the queue for the Hungarian chimney cakes at the Kürtősh booth wound around the corner. A busker in a Gumby suit played *Waltzing Matilda* on a marimba made out of PVC pipe.

Louisa and I had taken the train to this part of the city,

debarking at Kings Cross station and strolling the rest of the way, led by the app on Louisa's phone and sheer luck. I had to admit I was not at all sure where we were in the busy city and trusted that my well-traveled companion could get us home.

"Do you think she'll show up?" Louisa asked.

I nodded. "The stalker? I feel sure that she will. If nothing else, the latest note under Lily's door was an escalation of the threat." The note had referred to Rome, but I wasn't at all confident that Lily's nemesis wasn't here in Sydney. We couldn't take that chance.

We paused about a half block from the festivities, where we went over the few facts we knew. City police were on hand, as at most large public events, and there were private security guards specifically tasked with watching over Lily, in addition to escorts provided by her publisher. Our job was to watch for the vaguely familiar figure and sound the alert if we spotted her anywhere near our author.

Louisa squeezed my arm and pointed out a couple of landmarks. "The tall concrete building there, with the Aldi store—it's fairly visible. And across the street is that flagpole with the red banner flying. Let's meet at the flagpole every thirty minutes or so."

I nodded agreement. Was I keeping tabs on her, or was it the other way around? Didn't matter. Neither of us wanted to lose the other in this crowd.

She started directly into the fray ahead, while I peeled off to the right. I kept to the border of the chaos, a paper coffee cup in my left hand, and my right thumb worrying the zipper tab on my jacket. The look was deliberate: nondescript, American, possibly a little lost, a person you'd expect to see at any outdoor event, fairly invisible. My job was not to be spotted.

Within a few minutes, I came into the section designated for fans of the literary. Lily's tent was set up at the far end of the author corral, beyond the cluster of blue-and-white umbrellas designated for publisher signings. The banner above her table said, "Lily Davenport—Bestselling Author of *The Fifth Journey.*" A queue of well over fifty people stood there, waiting their turns.

She was seated behind a pyramid of hardcovers, her pen rarely pausing for a moment or two. Every so often, she'd look up and say something charming to the next in line, and you could see the fan—usually a woman in a tracksuit, sometimes a starstruck teenager—light up with joy. Lily had that effect; she wore fame the way some people wear cashmere, effortlessly and with class.

One would never guess from her demeanor what she was going through. And that, I supposed, was the true mark of a professional.

I counted the queue, which had lengthened. The event staff had set up a tape line on the ground, and two volunteers were managing the flow like junior flight attendants, checking receipts and keeping the fans from dominating the bestselling author's time. I watched them rotate through the routine: book, smile, signature, photo, shuffle. The engine of celebrity commerce, humming at optimal rpm.

I leaned against the trunk of a ghost gum and let my gaze slip over the scene, the way a lifeguard watches a crowded pool—not looking for the swimmers, but for the motion that doesn't fit. I spotted Louisa browsing a table of candle warmers, except that her eyes weren't on the merchandise.

The first circuit of the grounds took fifteen minutes.

I consulted my phone, pretending to text while my eyes mapped the boundaries of the event. Three security guards on perimeter—two with earpieces, one near the beer tent, doing his best to blend in. Two city cops standing near a coffee vendor's booth, chatting with each other while monitoring the crowd.

The event staff were volunteers, mostly uni students in fluorescent vests, invested only to the extent of keeping up with their friends. Overall, the threat level as a practical matter, seemed nil. Light security, the kind that deters the odd purse-snatcher, was evident but not the kind that plans for letter bombs or obsessed fans. Lily's publisher had done a good job of meeting our request for extra eyes on their star author.

The signature line thinned as I circled back. Most of the other authors were either sitting alone at their tables or had two or three fans awaiting signatures. Lily's line only increased with the passing minutes. Her hands moved faster, but she kept up the energy. No outward sign of nerves, though I knew from our talk that morning that her right foot would be tapping under the table, invisible to everyone else.

I let myself drift closer, weaving through the crowd until I could hear the exact timbre of Lily's voice. She'd dialed her smile up half a notch. She was a pro, but the mask slipped every so often. When a particularly effusive fan clutched her hand and started crying, Lily's eyes flicked to mine for a half-second, her mouth locked in a perfect "help me" smile.

I ignored it. Her publicity team were there to handle emotional fans; I couldn't allow myself to get sucked into that particular drama.

That's when I saw the woman.

She was standing inside the second ring of vendor stalls, half-shadowed by the awning of a donut cart, pretending to study a display of artisanal preserves. She wore that familiar navy coat—a touch too formal for the occasion—and a pair of sunglasses that covered half her face. The glasses were not fashion, but function, big enough to hide most of the upper cheek and brow, mirrored in the corners. Her hair was pinned in a loose chignon, and her posture was slightly hunched, as if she wanted to disappear.

But she gave off a jittery vibe. Nervous. I knew she was the one.

Chapter 18

The auburn-haired young woman almost spoiled everything.

The woman in the blue coat spotted her, hair pulled up in a high ponytail, wearing jeans and a fleece jacket, obviously American. Not security, exactly. Not law enforcement. She'd been at several of Lily's events, asking questions afterward, poking about where she had no right.

But the woman in the blue coat intuited more about this American than anyone would guess. She wasn't stupid. She knew things. Things her dull, bureaucratic daughter never gave her credit for. Resentment rose, but before it could take hold, she dropped her gaze and retreated two steps deeper into the shade cast by a tall concrete building.

She pretended to study a rack of tie-dyed scarves, ignoring the vendor's polite "Can I help you?" while keeping the American in her peripheral vision. The trick was to become scenery. Not invisible—no one is truly invisible at a street fair, not with the deliberate brightness of every pop-up tent, the shrieks of children jacked on sugar, and the jostle of tourists. She hadn't, however, anticipated that her long wool coat was rather dressy for the occasion, where everyone seemed to be in jeans or athleisure wear. She debated abandoning the coat, but that wasn't practical. The winter day could turn cold on short notice.

No matter. She had learned over time how not to stand out, how to slow her breathing to match the rhythm of the crowd, how to become the sort of figure that the eye skims over. She removed her sunglasses and stood in the midst of the crowd, half-shaded by a display of hand-woven blankets, and let herself be ignored.

From her vantage, the tent with the blue-and-gold banner stood in plain view. On a whim, she pulled her phone from her bag. A photo of her adversary would be a reminder of this event, something she could use. There, framed by stacks of hardcovers and a draped Australian flag, sat Lily Davenport herself. Beside her, the queue snaked out into the open, a procession of eager and starstruck fans, each one clutching a copy of *The Fifth Journey* to their chest as if it were a dear treasure.

Four other authors had tables and stacks of books. Lily, however, drew the crowd. Those others, the ignored ones, they must be seething. She knew the feeling.

She fumbled a moment with the camera app on the phone, technology she rarely used, and raised it, watching for the perfect shot. Lily's face did not betray the strain, not in any perceptible way. But her watcher saw it. The micro-breaks in the smile. The way the hand would clench the barrel of the pen after every inscription, whitening the knuckles. She quickly snapped two photos.

The author's occasional glance toward her escorts demonstrated the strain of being not only brilliant but also perfectly human, and yet not at all like the fans themselves. One after another, they babbled their small talk—Thank you for coming, You're such an inspiration, My sister shared your books with me—and Lily, the star, would tilt her head, flash a smile, and say some variation of "That means the world to me." Not once did she miss the cue; not once did she let the smile falter.

The woman in the blue coat felt a new flash of intense jealousy. This time the phone camera jittered when she pressed the button, blurring the image.

Then—there it was. A woman in the line, middle-aged with fluffy blonde hair, nervous, said her name softly as the book was handed over. The author's eyes flickered for a quarter-second, the mask slipped, revealing an instant of impatience. When she wrote the dedication, her hand wobbled slightly before resuming the calibrated posture of celebrity.

It was everything. The woman in the coat felt the jolt of satisfaction at her opponent's weakness. Weeks of watching, at many events, but this—this microsecond of fracture—she would replay over and over in her mind.

She shifted her weight, careful not to draw attention, dropped her phone into her pocket, and adjusted the position of her bag. The familiar presence of the notebook was inside, its tape-repaired spine frayed and its margins dense with her own scrawl.

Reaching up to touch her hair, she hoped the distinctive gray at her temples was adequately covered by the quick dye job she'd performed last night in her room. Had the American spotted her? Probably not. The nosy woman and her elder companion had been at several of Lily's events, but had not seen her yet; she felt fairly sure of that and loved the power of her own anonymity.

The book tent had become a hive, with the organizers buzzing nervously along the edges, intent upon keeping the queues moving.

She gripped the bag tighter and watched as a pair of teen girls at the front of the line posed for a selfie with the famous author, holding up her book, touching her hand in a gesture that would look warm and spontaneous in any photo. The girls squealed and ran off, broadcasting the moment to their social media followers.

A rush of bitterness swept through her, so sharp it left the woman dizzy. This scenario, this degree of adoration—it belonged to *her*, not to Ms. Lily *Davenport*. She wanted to scream with frustration. She let herself imagine what it would be like to approach the table and hand over her own book, to look the author in the eye and say, you know me, *thief*. She banished the thought as quickly as it appeared. There would be catharsis in a public scene, but not here. The audience for it wasn't right.

The next in line was a man, perhaps late thirties, who had the shambling affect of a person unused to being noticed. She saw a flicker of something in the author's face then—perhaps a touch of fear? He held out his book, and the author made eye contact, smile ready, but he only nodded and mumbled his thanks before fleeing.

The woman smirked. Lily had not yet identified the sender of the notes, and the not-knowing frightened her. She was afraid of everyone now. Good.

These tiny victories were satisfying, but she wanted the confession, the acknowledgment. She wanted to see Lily's face as she finally understood the pain caused by what she'd done.

There would be a final note, one last nudge to bring the memory bubbling to the surface. She began composing the next message in her mind. This time, she thought, Lily would surely remember. And then, in Rome, it would all end.

She strolled casually down the street, planning the train ride back to her hotel, scheming how to best deliver the next message. And that's when she spotted the American. The auburn-haired woman was focused directly on her.

Chapter 19

I caught movement and saw someone in a blue coat lift a smartphone and aim it in Lily's direction, not bothering to hide the movement. But every bit as quickly, she lowered it and seemed intent on the price of lilly pilly jam.

I was at least fifty feet away, with lots of people in between, but she might fit our profile. Forty to fifty, northern European facial structure but with a tightness around the mouth, although the hair was somewhat different. She appeared to be taking pictures of Lily. Paparazzi? But she didn't quite have the look of that.

She could simply be a fan who liked to catch candid shots when Lily was distracted by conversation. Still, it was odd that she never actually entered the signing tent. She didn't seem to be here for an autograph. A security volunteer ambled by with a clipboard, and the woman ducked behind the donut cart.

This was not regular fandom, but I couldn't be certain.

I edged my way closer, past the donut cart, eyeing a table of ceramics as an excuse, and caught her reflection in the vendor's display mirror. Her hands were bare—no gloves. She scanned her phone twice, then turned and re-anchored on Lily.

I pulled out my own phone, held it low, and snapped a shot of the woman as she took a picture. But she moved at the last second, and I only caught the edge of her shoulder. I felt an odd animal sense that sometimes you watch the watcher and find out they're two steps ahead.

She clocked me eventually. Her face didn't so much as flicker. She dropped her phone into her pocket and casually turned away. I could be completely wrong about this one.

I spotted Louisa near Lily's table, where the signing queue was down to stragglers—one girl with a skate helmet, a young mother shepherding identical twins in matching Hogwarts sweatshirts, and a few others. Lily handled them with efficiency, each signature punctuated with a "there you are, darling," and a ready smile.

I cut through the crowd to Lily's tent, leaned over her shoulder, and dropped my voice to a murmur. Louisa came in close to us. "You've got a photographer. Navy coat, east side of the road, was watching you for several minutes. Louisa, did you see her?"

"I'm so sorry. I must have let my attention wander to the people in the book signing line."

The event staff had also relaxed; one was scrolling TikTok, the other was fixing the tape line with her shoe.

Lily didn't break stride. She signed the book for the young mom, posed for a selfie, and only after the family had moved on did she look up at me with a smile so stiff it could have doubled as a mask. She set her pen down, hands flat in her lap. "Is it her?"

I hesitated. "I really don't know. The coat and sunglasses seemed like a giveaway, but aside from snapping a couple of photos in your general direction, she didn't show much interest."

She exhaled once, short and sharp. "I have a half hour to go."

"She was over in the food area. I'll tail her, and I'll alert the hired security guys," I said. "If she comes close, Louisa, you cut her off. Lily, you finish here, then we'll regroup."

Lily nodded, picked up her pen, and gestured for the next in line.

At the edge of the event, beyond the temporary fencing, was a taxi stand and a row of portable toilets. No blue coat there. Then, as I pivoted to scan the southern entrance, I caught a sliver of navy beyond the fence.

She was outside the fair, standing near a battered park bench, pretending to read a city map, but every so often she'd raise her head, eyes glued toward Lily's table.

I considered calling the event security, but it would be a waste of time. The woman wasn't breaking any laws, and she'd vanish the moment anyone in a vest walked toward her.

Well, there was one thing I could do—confront the woman. If she truly was the one sending the notes, I'd get it out of her, find out her motives, and I'd ... I'd ... I didn't know exactly what, but the police could take it from there.

I turned around with the intention of marching right up to that park bench and calling her out on her behavior. But the bench was empty, and there was no sign of the woman near it. She'd spotted me. I ducked through the street barricades for the fair, dodged between two parked cars, and ran to the bench.

If she was a pro, she'd know to avoid a straight line and would not bolt unless she had cover. I spotted a delivery access road behind the market and headed that way. I circled the canvas maze and jogged the fifty meters to the service alley, my shoes sticking to the spilled soda and old chewing gum that paved the way.

At the mouth of the alley, a delivery truck blocked half the lane, its hazard lights pulsing. I craned around the cab, peered through the windshield, and saw nothing but the driver, slouched over his phone, oblivious to the drama outside his steel cocoon. I slid past the truck, careful not to lose my footing on the curb, and emerged onto the quiet side street that ran parallel to the market.

A block ahead, I caught sight of the navy-blue coat. The woman was walking briskly—certainly not at a run—doing her best to appear the same as anyone else out on a nice afternoon. I picked up my pace. I'd closed about half the distance when she heard the slap of my trainers on the sidewalk. She spun and took off running.

At the corner, she made a sharp left turn. A block of upscale row houses stood across the road on the right, but the woman had taken a downhill path to the left. By the time I caught up, I realized she'd gone into a small park with a plaque bearing the name of it, but I was concentrating too hard on keeping sight of the blue coat to read it.

The terrain was steep, and I bounded down two sets of steps carved into the hillside, with short logs inset to keep the soil from eroding away. This was similar to a botanical garden, but much wilder and freer than the formal gardens we'd toured. Huge trees towered toward each other, blocking the sky, and the shady path led to interesting little alcoves with an occasional table and chairs, a bench here and there. Ahead, it was impossible to tell what waited around the next curve, but I kept running, trying to avoid an unexpected drop-off.

At one of the small benches, I noticed a gray-haired man with a book on his lap. He was staring up toward the highest trees.

"Sir, did you happen to see a woman in a long blue coat pass this way?" My breath was coming in gasps.

"Kookaburra," he said, pointing upward, clearly not understanding my question.

I repeated it, but the man shrugged, and the bird in the tree let out an eerie cackle, mocking me. I jogged on, feeling closed in by the dense foliage, seeing no other people.

My quarry either knew the park well, or she got lucky in choosing the correct forks in the path to lose me. By the time I'd been in there ten minutes, I was at least three stories below street level and discovered I'd traveled in a massive loop. When I spotted the upward trail for the way I'd come down, I decided I'd better take it. A person not wanting to be found in this tiny jungle could dodge behind endless trees or into all sorts of cubbyholes.

My bruised ego and I managed to return to the street fair intact. I circled through, found Lily finishing up her last signature, and told her and Louisa what I'd done. "I have no idea whether she's still in the maze of that little garden, or if she could have made her way back here."

Lily's voice was steady, but her hands shook as she capped the pen. "I'm going to have to walk out of here, aren't I?"

"Not alone," I said. "Stay behind the event staff, and

I'll tail you both. If she gets close, I'll take care of it."

Lily smiled, faint and crooked.

We walked together to the exit, Lily bracketed by two volunteers, me in the rear. I checked every shadow, every car, every face. The woman in the navy coat was nowhere to be seen.

As we reached the rideshare zone, Lily turned to me. "She'll be at the hotel, won't she?"

"Possibly. Have your escorts see you safely inside, and check with the desk to see if anyone's been asking about you."

I glanced around for the navy-coated woman. No sign of her. We waited in silence. When Lily's car arrived, I opened the door, watched her slide in, along with the two publisher escorts. I leaned down to catch her eye. "Text me when you're in. Triple lock the door."

She smiled, this time with effort. "You make a very good bodyguard."

The car pulled away, taillights vanishing down the hill. Louisa had caught up, and she asked me whether I'd seen the woman after leaving the garden.

I shook my head. "Nada. It seemed like that woman anticipated my every move, knew every shortcut, and left only the ghost of herself behind."

"Darling, you do have some experience with ghosts, you know." I immediately thought of the cemetery in Bury St. Edmunds.

There was nothing to do now but catch the train to our own part of the city.

Chapter 20

Satisfied that she had indeed eluded the persistent American, the woman found a bench beneath a jacaranda tree and opened her notebook. She reviewed her notes, savoring and underlining every instance of the author's anxiety, circling the times she'd seen the American woman at close range. She tore out a fresh page and, with a fountain pen identical to the one used for the notes, drafted the next message:

Dear Lily,
The presence of hunters at your side will not absolve you.
You will find no sanctuary in crowds, or in the care of strangers.
You know where this ends.
A.

She reread the note until she was satisfied. She would carefully copy the message onto her special stationery, address an envelope, and arrange for its delivery in the next city, in the usual way. By the time of her arrival in Rome, she would be fully ready.

Chapter 21

We woke the next morning with no specific plans, something that seemed like an oversight. Lily had a talk scheduled at the library in the afternoon, followed by her publisher's party. We'd shopped ourselves out, and the sights were beginning to look alike, so I wasn't sure whether all this empty time was a good thing. Lily must have been thinking along the same lines.

Her text said she'd heard from the Finch & Fig, the bookshop where she'd signed books the first day. They'd received stock of the new book and several of her backlist titles and were wondering if she could make time to stop by, informally, and sign them. She'd agreed and now wondered whether I thought it would be a good idea for Louisa and me to go along with her.

It wouldn't be a bad idea, I decided. We agreed to meet

in an hour's time.

I showed Louisa the chain of texts. "If you have other plans, I can certainly go by myself," I told her.

But she positively bubbled at the thought of returning to the shop. "I saw a lovely journal when I was there, and I've been thinking ever since that I should have bought it. Might we go a little early and pick up a few pastries at that coffee place next to it?"

Another thing we'd both developed a craving for here in Sydney were the fine quality patisserie creations we kept spotting in bakery windows. She didn't have to twist my arm.

It wasn't a long walk to The Rocks, where we found a café that screamed our names. The sun was out and it seemed like the perfect morning to grab an outdoor table and treat ourselves to coffee and pastry. We got lucky when an elderly couple vacated a table and we were the first in line for it. We took seats under a blue umbrella and placed our orders.

"Keep an eye out for Lily," I suggested. "She might like to join us."

My *mille fuille* and Louisa's mini *rhum baba* arrived on dainty plates, each with a dessert fork. As I was stirring a dollop of cream into my coffee, a colorful bird caught my eye. Larger than a parakeet but smaller than a cockatiel, his plumage was a rainbow—vivid sections of purple, yellow, green, red, and orange. As I watched, he landed on the umbrella above the table next to ours and strutted to the very edge of it. Eyeing the tables below, he cocked his head, looking for something specific. I was afraid it was my pastry, so I scooted my plate closer to my arm.

Louisa was enthralled, as the bird spread his wings and floated down to the top of another table. He marched up to the plastic container of sweeteners and proceeded to pick through them. When he found what he wanted—natural sugar, none of that artificial stuff—he plucked two of the packets from the container and carried them up to his spot on the umbrella. I could see only enough of him to know he was ripping the end off the packet and slurping the contents.

"It's a lorikeet," said a voice I recognized.

Lily had spotted us and walked over while we were entertained by the bird show.

"In nature they love the nectar of certain flowers, but when humans are around, they're perfectly happy to share our sweets." She placed an arm around Louisa's shoulders and nodded toward the pastry on her plate. "May I join you?"

"Absolutely. We were hoping we'd see you." I relaxed in my chair, holding my mug and watching as the lorikeet flipped the empty sugar wrapper to the ground, scoped out another table, and helped himself to another.

Lily sat, declining either coffee or pastry, saying she'd had her fill at the Windsor. We exchanged pleasantries, establishing that everyone had slept well despite the sighting of the woman in the blue coat yesterday at the street fair.

"Perhaps you frightened her away for good," Louisa offered, "chasing her into the woods as you did."

I doubted it, but let a mouthful of my pastry save me from expressing that thought.

I spotted a glimmer of auburn hair and recognized Hazel from the Finch & Fig, striding down the lane toward us, and I waved her over.

She took the fourth chair. "I had to get out of the shop

for a few," she said, "the manager is in one of his moods. Besides, it's time for my break."

"Can I treat you to a coffee?"

She waved the offer away. "I won't be long. I just—" She broke off, glanced at her hands, and seemed to do a mood reset.

Lily shifted in her seat. "Is this a bad time for me to go in and sign stock?"

"Oh, no, not at all. You are the one person who would definitely improve Mr. Welles's mood."

Louisa had pushed her empty plate aside and drained the last of her coffee. "I'll walk over with you. Together we'll charm him right out of that mood."

I looked over at Hazel. "Do you need to get—"

"No, we're fine. I have fifteen minutes and I'm taking it all." She watched as the two older ladies walked away. "Charlie, I was hoping to catch a moment with you. After you came in, asking about anyone who might be stalking Ms. Davenport, I..."

Her hands fidgeted in her lap.

Rather than reveal that I thought we had our stalker, I waited for her to come out with whatever she knew.

"Okay. Here's the thing. After you left, I remembered something."

"Go on."

"There's a gentleman," she said, her voice sliding into the octave reserved for secrets. "Gregor Anton. He's been at every Lily signing in Sydney for the last three years, and I mean *every* one. Often first in line, sometimes brings flowers, sometimes only the books. But always there."

"A superfan."

Hazel nodded, relief creeping into her posture now

that she'd gotten the words out. "The thing is, he's not, like, dangerous? I mean, he's never done anything except get books signed. And he's polite. But it's the volume—like, he'll buy six copies at a time. Different printings. He says he's collecting, but nobody needs that many unless they're running a black-market eBay empire, and he isn't."

Could I have been completely wrong about the woman suspect? "Did he ever say anything odd to Lily? Or about her?"

Hazel ran her fingers through her short hair, setting it on end. "He's intense, but not aggressive. More like, I don't know, worshipful. When he speaks to her during the bookstore events, it's like he's practiced the conversation a hundred times. He quoted her book to her. Like, full paragraphs, word for word. Lily was gracious about it, but you could tell she was a little freaked."

I had to admit, the behavior was unusual. "Did he ever ask about her tour schedule? Or for any personal details?"

"Not to me," Hazel said. "But he's in all the social media fan groups, so he probably knows more about her than her publisher does."

I let that sit for a minute, watching Hazel wind down from her initial burst of adrenaline. "Do you think he's capable of sending threatening notes?"

Hazel's face did a quick shuffle—surprise, contemplation, then a slow response. "He's harmless ... I think."

But sometimes people who are harmless simply haven't had the right provocation. What if the woman in the dark coat was merely a courier, delivering messages on behalf of a man who might have entirely different intentions toward Lily? His last name did begin with an A.

"Do you have contact details for him?"

Hazel nodded. "He comes to the store nearly every week, so he's on our mailing list. But I can text him and set up a meeting." She hesitated. "Do you want me there? Or do you want to do this on your own?"

I considered. "Better if you can introduce us. He trusts you."

"Okay. I can tell him you're a journalist. Or a researcher?"

"Researcher is fine. Is it doable for this afternoon?"

Hazel checked her phone, then her watch, which had Spider-Man for a face. Her thumbs fired off a quick text. "I'll let you know what he says if you want to give me your number."

"Perfect," I said, and pushed my card across the table. "If anything weird happens, call me. Day or night."

Hazel took the card, slipped it into her phone case. "It's fun watching you," she said. "You make it seem like no big deal, but I can tell you're three steps ahead."

I smiled. Sometimes it pays to let people believe what they want.

Hazel stood. Her phone chimed with a text. "Looks like he's on board, so I'll see you at three this afternoon."

"Thanks, Hazel. You did the right thing, and hopefully I can learn something helpful from this customer of yours."

She nodded and headed in the direction of Finch & Fig.

I sat back, processing. Gregor. It had the right ring to it, the right amount of eccentricity. The *worshipful* detail worried me a little. It can be a fine line between adoration and obsession.

I shook the thought off, pulled out my phone, and dialed Louisa.

She answered on the first ring, and I told her about my conversation with Hazel, about Gregor, about the planned meeting.

"Do you want me there?" she asked, a little too quickly.

"He's more likely to open up if it's only me. Besides, I was thinking you might attend Lily's talk at the library this afternoon. If you want to?"

She sounded delighted.

This afternoon, I'd meet Gregor. I gathered my things, paid for the desserts and coffees, and stepped out of the lane, feeling the wind off the harbor cut straight through my jacket.

Chapter 22

I got to the Finch & Fig forty minutes ahead of schedule, which gave me time to re-read the threatening letters, this time considering them from the perspective of whether a man might be the sender. I couldn't be absolutely sure. Plus, it never hurts to cross all the t's.

Gregor arrived precisely at the top of the hour, opening the glass door a little hesitantly. He paused on the threshold, scanning the main room. When he spotted Hazel, he gave a little wave. They exchanged a brief, slightly awkward greeting, and she led him to me.

Gregor was thinner than I'd pictured, his body language a series of rapid-fire tics: clutching and releasing the messenger bag, adjusting his wire-rimmed glasses with a two-fingered jab, constantly checking the line of his sleeve. Immediately, I dismissed him as the person in the long blue coat and wide hat, who was nowhere near this fidgety and not the same build. Still, it didn't mean he wasn't involved somehow.

He wore a button-down shirt with the collar open, but the cuffs were tightly fastened. His messenger bag, slung across his torso, was battered and covered with an array of literary pins and buttons—Obscure Reference, Bad Grammar Police, Read Banned Books.

Hazel made the introductions. "Gregor, this is Charlotte. She's visiting from the States—Albuquerque, right? She's a friend of Lily Davenport's."

Gregor's eyes went wide behind the glasses, his face animating in a way I could only describe as hopeful. "Albuquerque, the *Breaking Bad* place?"

"That's the one," I said with a tight smile. A lot of us aren't exactly thrilled with the image given to our city in the TV series.

Hazel laughed and excused herself to go and shelve some books.

Gregor unslung his bag, fished out a stack of trade paperbacks, and arranged them on the table. "You came here for Lily's tour, then?"

"In a sense," I said. "My aunt has known Lily for years. They worked together, briefly, at a summer program." And then I lied a little. "She mentioned you in passing, said you were one of her most loyal readers."

Gregor beamed at that, a full-wattage smile. "She's amazing. Her work—it gets better and better. Did you know she's got a new book in progress? Her publisher keeps teasing us about it, but she won't say anything to us directly. I've been to every signing, every Q&A."

Exactly as Hazel had told me, and his social feeds—

public, for the most part—confirmed it. Every event tagged with over-the-top praise, every reading recapped in exquisite detail.

I glanced at the stack. There were six copies of the same book, all different editions. One was in German, which, as it turned out, Gregor didn't speak. "So, you're a collector?" I asked.

He looked a little embarrassed. "I guess? I … each printing is a little different, sometimes the cover art, sometimes the description. I like to have them all."

"May I?" I asked, picking up the US edition.

"Please," he said, and slid the rest closer.

I flipped through. Gregor had made notes on sticky tabs, scribbled observations, page cross-references. I took my time with each note, checking for a match to the threatening notes, but his handwriting was radically different—precise penmanship, the letter "f" crossed with a faint line, the loops of the lowercase letters neatly closed. The ink was black, from an ordinary ballpoint pen. The notes that Lily had received were in blue ink, block letters, aggressive. Not a match.

Hazel watched the exchange, her body language wary. I handed the book back to Gregor. "You've got a real eye for detail," I said. "Did you ever want to write?"

He made a sound—half laugh, half groan. "I tried, but I couldn't finish anything. I like reading better. It's less stressful."

"Sometimes being a great reader is a bigger commitment than being a writer," I said, which drew a tiny, involuntary smile from Hazel.

Gregor gave me a quizzical look. "So, um, what did you want to talk about?"

I decided to be honest with him. "Hazel said you were the resident expert on all things Lily. We're trying to find a person who sent Lily a disturbing note. I was hoping you could tell me about the local scene. Who comes to the signings, any odd stories, things like that."

Gregor nodded, launching into a spiel about the regulars—young mums, middle-aged housewives, students, the occasional guy. "Like me, I guess. There are a few hangers-on, the groupies, but most only want a signed book and a photo. Sometimes people bring gifts—chocolates, wine. I recall a mug once that said World's Best Writer."

"Has anything ever happened at a signing that felt *off*?" I asked. "Anyone aggressive or inappropriate?"

"Oh, no. I'd have stepped in."

Lily's personal guard, I sensed a genuine protectiveness here. "How about someone who seemed too intent, too watchful?"

He shook his head, thinking. "No, not really. I mean, there's often someone who tries to monopolize her time. She's very patient, but the event staff are good at moving the line. I did hear that someone sent her a weird letter last year, but I don't know what it said. She talked about receiving strange questions from fans, but only in vague terms and with bits of humor inserted."

"Did she say who sent it, the weird letter?"

"No, nothing like that. I got the impression it had been a one-time thing."

I tucked that away. "If you were her, would you feel safe on this tour?"

Gregor considered, taking his time with the question. "She's a public figure. I'm sure she has to be careful. But I don't think anyone's out to get her. People love her. If there was a real threat, they'd tell us, right? Many of us—I, for one—would do anything to keep her safe in such a situation."

"She would appreciate that," I said, not wanting to get into details. "I'm sure you're right about the threat."

Hazel checked her watch and looked across the room at Gregor with a small, conspiratorial grin. "I think Charlotte's working on a secret biography."

Gregor lit up, delighted at the idea. "I can help with that. I've archived every interview she's ever given, including the deleted ones. There's a fan page for those—sometimes the moderators take them down for copyright, but I've got PDFs."

"Could you send me a few links?" I asked. He rattled off an email address (GregorReads, naturally), and I keyed it into my phone.

The conversation drifted to Lily's next appearance, then to the "hidden codes" Gregor believed she tucked into every book—a theory that, while slightly manic, was more enthusiastic than sinister.

"One last question, and I'll let you go," I said, as casually as I could. "Have you ever written to her? Like, actual letters, not only on social media?"

He shook his head, face open and guileless. "I wouldn't want to bother her. She must be incredibly busy and is probably sick of people."

I believed him. The loneliness in his answer rang as true as anything I'd heard all week.

Gregor packed up his books, zipping the messenger bag carefully as he stood. Before leaving, he turned and said, "If you see Lily, tell her we're all rooting for her. And that the new book doesn't have to be perfect. We'll love it, no matter what."

I promised I would.

He walked out the door, his shadow stretching across the polished floor as the sun dipped behind the bridge.

I said goodbye to Hazel, thanking her for facilitating the meeting. As I left the shop, I let my mind sift through the interview. Gregor was no stalker. If anything, he was the type of fan writers wished for—devoted and hungry for the next story. His handwriting was completely different from the threatening notes. His knowledge of Lily was extensive but all available online, and he never once asked me for information that wasn't already public.

I took a moment to text Louisa: Gregor = harmless. Obsessive but not dangerous. Handwriting doesn't match.

She replied: Disappointed but not surprised. Back to the original theory?

Yes. To the notes. Still think the tone feels less 'fan' and more 'peer.' How's the library event going?

Louisa sent a string of thoughtful emojis, then: Good. I'll fill you in at dinner tonight?

Absolutely! Suggest a place, I'm open.

She sent me the address and link to a pizza place in Erskineville, of all places. But she had raved about the tiny place the day she went on her adventure trek to Sydney Park, so I figured why not get out and see something different than the city center. I dropped my phone into my bag and walked toward the train station.

Studying the route, I figured out what to do and tapped my Opal card to get on. The train was full of homeward-bound commuters, most staring at phones or out the windows. Conversation was practically nonexistent.

I pulled out my notebook and went through my

observations from the whole week, glancing up each time the train slowed to be sure I didn't miss my stop.

First things first: I ruled out Gregor. His handwriting bore no resemblance to the notes, his manner was too open, too eager. Even his obsessive fandom followed the rules of etiquette; he'd not asked about Lily's hotel, never pressed for access. He was simply a person who wanted to belong and found a home in Lily's books.

I double-checked everything anyway. Photos of the threat notes were on my phone in the order they'd arrived. The verbiage was nothing like the way Gregor spoke. Once again, I didn't get the feeling this was a fan obsessed to the point of being dangerous. I hadn't seriously considered him a suspect once I realized he couldn't be the person in the long coat, but I know from experience that it's important to check every suspect, verify every clue. Especially since we would be leaving Sydney soon.

The pattern in the notes was obviously about escalation—upping the ante, making each contact personal, and darker. Whoever was sending these knew Lily's movements, but also, they knew her vulnerabilities. The references in the notes were to the past: "debts unpaid," "the August sky," "the journey's end."

Back to my notebook, I came across the note I'd scribbled the night before: "Not a fan. Peer? Old rival?" If I trusted my gut, the writer was someone who had personally known Lily in the past.

The mechanical voice on the train announced my station, so I dropped everything into my bag and made my way to the doors. The crowd moved as a flow, with me in the middle. Belatedly, I remembered that I had to tap off or I'd be billed for the length of the trip to the end of the line. I rummaged in my pocket for the Opal card and tapped it on the tiny scanner.

Following the flow of human movement, I came out on the street and briefly stepped aside to figure out where I needed to go next. Thank goodness for Google Maps and verbal instructions.

Ten minutes later, I spotted the corner pizzeria. Louisa was right—the place was miniscule with only four tables. I was early enough to have a choice, and I grabbed one, ordering a Coke to avoid attracting glares while I waited. It soon became clear that the bulk of their business was take-away, as one Uber Eats person after another walked in and picked up pizza boxes. The scents coming out of the kitchen were definitely making me salivate.

I spent the next ten minutes reviewing the photos Louisa had sent me from the street fair book signing—every fan in the line, every bystander. She'd caught a better shot than my feeble attempt of the woman in the navy coat, her mirrored sunglasses hiding everything but the set of her jaw. I didn't know her name, but my case file for her was growing. She was meticulous, deliberate, and possibly the most patient person I'd ever tracked. I had no clue why she hadn't yet approached Lily face-to-face. But I was ninety-nine percent sure she was the one who had eluded me in the tiny secret garden.

Louisa arrived exactly when she said she would, tartan scarf fluttering in the wind. She spotted me through the window and joined me. We spent a couple of minutes deciding on what to order.

Once the food question was settled, she looked over at my open notebook. "So, Gregor?"

"Total dead end. His handwriting is in a different universe, and he's incapable of subtlety. If he wanted to send a threat, he'd probably hand-deliver it on a gold platter and stammer as he asked Lily to read it."

Louisa chuckled. "You do realize you sound almost disappointed?"

"I wanted him to be the one. He probably would have willingly confessed and the police could have hauled him away. Case closed."

She nodded. "So, the next theory?"

"I'm thinking we're back to what we talked about before—that it's not a fan at all. Whoever it is, they're invested in Lily, but not in the way that gets you a signed copy and a selfie. This is personal, and the timing fits the arc of her career—when she really gets to the big time, the notes start. First in the UK, and now following her along her tour. It's like they're trying to chase her across the globe, reminding her that no matter how far she goes, she can't outrun something from the past."

Louisa glanced at my photo of one of the notes. "This line—'debts are not paid by silence'—that's somewhat literary."

"Exactly. It's a threat, but it's also a message. I'd bet you anything it's someone from her old writing circle, or a disgruntled colleague." I met Louisa's eyes. "Go back over it with me. Did she ever mention any enemies?"

"Nothing recent. But she did say that early on, when her very first book broke out, someone accused her of stealing a plot or a character. Her publisher's legal team apparently got right on it, and it went nowhere. She briefly mentioned it during the workshop I attended, but she seemed reluctant to discuss details."

"Do you think this is revenge?"

She shrugged. The young server brought our pizza, and we shifted into the routine of passing paper plates and napkins across the table before each grabbing a slice.

We finished the pizza in silence, the comfortable kind, although I kept mulling over the idea of revenge. It fit the MO; the messages becoming more pointed with each new contact.

By the time we finished eating, it was dark outside. Louisa stood and bundled her scarf around her neck while I zipped my jacket, and we stepped out to the sidewalk, getting our bearings for the walk to the train station.

"Rome is next," I said. "If we don't solve this before the tour is over, I'm not sure we ever will."

"You'll solve it," she said. "I have faith."

As we walked toward the corner, I caught a glimpse of my own reflection in the pizzeria window—tired, a little worn, but not ready to give up. I pulled my collar tight, and we headed down the softly lit street.

Chapter 23

Checking my email the following morning, I discovered Lily had sent me a folder of material from her 2017 workshop, with a note apologizing for taking so long to locate and copy the materials. "She must have been up late last night," I murmured as I opened the documents.

Louisa perched on the room's window seat, a patchwork of sunlight pooling at her feet, sipping ginger tea and watching the city in the soft morning light. She wore her hair up, wisps escaping to catch the light, and every so often she'd make a comment—mostly about the strangeness of Australian birds.

"I usually imagined detectives as night creatures," she said at one point, "but you do your best scheming when the sun's up."

"I like a well-lit crime," I quipped, sorting the files into alphabetical order. "Darkness is overrated."

She laughed, a good hearty one.

The workshop roster spreadsheet listed ten participants, all chosen through a competitive process that—according to what Lily had told me—was supposed to foster camaraderie rather than rivalry. The sheet included name, address, phone, email … standard data on each attendee. But in another column, the instructor added bits of opinion or observation, and a final column gave a few words of assessment of the work. Most were positive, but a few noted personality traits such as "condescending," "insecure but talented."

Then there were the workshop assignments themselves, marked with instructor comments. I cross-referenced each name with the corresponding feedback forms, looking for anything that would tie the student writer's work to the tone or style of the threatening letters.

I copied the spreadsheet into a new document so I could add my own notes without changing anything in Lily's original. Four of the ten participants had either a first or last initial letter A. I highlighted those in pale blue, realizing that our present-day stalker could choose any letter of the alphabet they wanted. *A* could stand for anarchist, for all I knew. But somehow I didn't think so.

Louisa set her teacup down and came to stand beside me and look over my shoulder. "Oh, how sweet," she said.

I followed her fingertip and saw her name on the roster. In the comment section, Lily had described Louisa as "cooperative" and her assessment noted "very talented with dialogue."

"I do recall she praised my dialogue sections. Didn't know she found me to be cooperative."

"And why wouldn't she? You really aren't much of a troublemaker." I sent a side-smile in her direction.

She pointed at one of my blue-highlighted names and ran her finger across the sheet to the assessment section. "A budding talent who needs much work."

"What is it?" I asked.

"There," she said at last, her voice gone precise and clipped. "That one. I remember her."

I checked the line: "A. Morris (Amelia)" with a notation "a little obsessive" in the same column where Louisa had been described as cooperative.

"You remember something about this person, don't you?"

Louisa drew in a measured breath, eyes narrowing. "She was—" Louisa paused, searching for the right word. "She was the sort who didn't smile unless someone else was failing. She'd give these critiques—rarely about the work, mostly about the person. Every time another student mentioned a publication accepting their work, even if a small one, she'd go rigid, as though their success was a personal insult to her. Her critiques were full of corrections and alternate endings. She wrote as if she and Lily were equals, or as if she was the teacher and Lily the student, rather than the other way round."

I scanned over the titles of the other documents, finding a feedback sheet for Morris. The folder contained eight documents, one for each week's assignment in the class. I opened the first one, in which the student had written a two-page character profile for a fictional protagonist. Lily's attached comments were highly positive. The second document was a similar profile for a fictional antagonist. Lily remained positive but pointed out that the antagonist needed stronger motive. I skimmed forward to assignment eight. Here, Lily offered a positive comment on the student's final story but suggested further work to deepen both major characters and to polish the ending to a satisfying conclusion.

Louisa had retreated to her bedroom while I did the reading, and when I called out to her, she emerged dressed for the day and with her hair freshly brushed.

"Recalling what you can about this person, how do you think she would have reacted to Lily's instructional comments on this?"

She read over my shoulder. "Hm, I don't quite know … I mean, the comments seem fair. Lily gave us ideas to help strengthen our writing. That was the entire purpose of taking the class, wasn't it? But Amelia Morris was different."

I thought of the personality notation, how this person probably obsessively wrote and rewrote a story until she believed it was perfect. She might not take kindly to being told the piece could use further work.

I looked at Louisa, who had drifted to the window seat and back. "Did she seem like a diligent student?" I asked.

Louisa nodded, lips pursed. "I don't recall her ever missing a single class in the eight weeks. But she was not very sociable. Sat in the back, never joined us for drinks after."

"Did she ever threaten anyone?" I asked.

"Not really," Louisa replied, her gaze distant, "but I remember once she told another student—one who'd recently landed an agent—something like, 'the world doesn't reward the derivative for long.' The way she said it … there was superiority in it, but also a kind of grief. As if she'd been cheated out of something she should have earned."

And phrased in a very literary manner.

"Did Lily ever have to intervene?"

Louisa nodded. "Once, at the midpoint. Amelia blew up, accused someone of stealing a line from her story. It wasn't proven to be the exact same line, but there was tension. After that, Lily made us all sign a code of conduct. Seemed a little absurd, but it calmed things."

I pulled up the digital folder, scanning for a copy of the code. There it was: *All participants must respect the work and privacy of others. Breaches may result in dismissal.* It sounded perfectly reasonable to me.

"Did you see Ms. Morris after the workshop ended?" I asked.

"No, come to think of it. Several of the rest of us would occasionally get together. Eventually, over the years, we all drifted apart."

I stared at the documents on my computer, wishing I had the original paper copies, feeling like I would learn more from them, especially if handwritten comments or notations had been added later.

"Louisa," I said, "do you remember if Amelia ever used special stationery? Handmade, heavy cream, A5? Similar to the notes Lily has recently received?"

She stared at me, her eyes wide. "I can't believe I hadn't recalled this. Amelia brought her own. Wouldn't use the group notepads, said they were too cheap for her taste. Actually, not A5 individual sheets, but she bought her own notebooks from some boutique in Notting Hill. She said the heavy paper and a fountain pen made her feel like a real writer. Of course, we were required to submit our final assignments as a Word document. Lily explained that was the format an agent or publisher would expect, and she wanted us presenting our work as professionals."

I brought up the purchase record Ellen had sent me from Pembroke's. "Five weeks ago, a woman bought twenty sheets of Regency A5, paid cash, refused to give her name. Wore gloves, large sunglasses, and a navy coat."

Louisa started to speak, but closed her mouth. I could see the moment the memory crystallized. "Yes. That's her. She wore navy a lot. And she often wore gloves when the weather was not terribly cold. Said she was allergic to many things, but I think she liked the ritual, the classy formality."

I felt the air in the room change, a realization around a single truth. Amelia Morris fit the age and appearance profile, and she may have felt slighted by Lily during the workshop. I felt sure we'd finally put a name to our suspect.

Louisa leaned in, eyes fixed on the page. "Is it really that simple?" she said, a note of hope coloring her words.

"It rarely is," I said, "but having a name gives us a direction. Putting on my psychologist hat, I would guess she's not a fan; she's a rival. Someone who wants the world to see her as Lily's equal, or better."

Louisa considered this, nodded as if she'd known the answer and needed it said aloud. "What now?"

I glanced at the clock. It was early in the day. I checked the event schedule. Lily's appearance in Rome was in less than seventy-two hours at the central library. If 'A' was following the tour, she'd be there—perhaps in the open, maybe lurking at the fringes. I jumped online and finalized the airline booking I'd reserved earlier.

"Now, we pack our bags."

Chapter 24

Rome, at last. And here in this ancient city she would stage the final showdown tomorrow!

She caught her reflection in the mirror of her tiny hotel room, a silhouette crowned by wild, static hair. At least her graying spots had been covered. She stood and paced, clutching a handful of her own work and a copy of Lily Davenport's novel.

Her notebook was open, the relevant page flagged with a sliver of sticky note—her own draft from the workshop, marked Session 8. She opened Lily's book to the page she'd marked and traced the margin with her left index finger, stopping at the key phrase—her phrase—lifted from her story and now parading through the fourth chapter of *The Fifth Journey*. She'd underlined it in blue, and copied the passage from Lily's novel onto the facing page of her notebook, the two versions staring at each other. Each time she saw them together, the pain was as fresh as when the theft had first occurred.

"It's nearly exact," she whispered, turning the last word into a snarl. She circled the line in the original, then in the copy, and connected them with a sharp, downward slash. "Not even subtle."

She flipped to the next section—the twist at the end, the protagonist's sudden, solitary exile. She'd conceived that moment on a rain-streaked bus from Cambridge, the words tumbling in her head until she could scribble them onto a receipt. And here it was, in print, on page 312 of the British edition—only the city had changed, and the protagonist wore a different coat. She ran her finger down the text, stabbing at the point of convergence with her pen.

"She stole everything. My characters. My plot twists. My life's work."

She read them side by side, first in a mumble, then louder, her voice cracking as she repeated the lines from her notebook: "A city of endless windows, each one a secret." And in *The Fifth Journey*: "She watched the city through the train window, every passing sight holding a secret."

She felt a moment's confusion in reading the words. Hadn't they been identical?

Yes, she was certain of it. Her anger bloomed and she scrawled a note in her own margin: And yet the world calls *her* a visionary.

She caught sight of her special stationery, its pale cream mocking her from the bed. Snatching a sheet of it, she slipped on the thin cotton gloves for handling the pages, and ran her fingers over the weight and grain. She remembered the moment of purchase in the Notting Hill shop, the clerk's gaze averted as she counted out cash. Had Lily ever known the pleasure of selecting her own materials, or had she been given everything by default?

Bringing the page to her nose, she inhaled the scent of the paper, sat at the desk, and uncapped her pen. For a long time, she stared at the blank sheet, preparing to write the words she had composed in the secret garden, hesitating.

She recapped the pen, set it down, and walked over to the window. When she began to speak, it was to rehearse the confrontation she would soon have with the author. "You think you're the only one who suffered? That I didn't pour my *life* into those drafts? You took what you wanted and left the rest of us to rot."

She imagined how it would play out in a courtroom when the time came, the rows of faceless critics and readers, the author perched on the stand, unable to explain how the stolen phrases had wormed their way into her text.

"Did you think no one would notice?" she said, her voice rising. "Or did you simply not care?"

On the bed were copies of *Publisher's Weekly* and *Library Journal*. She thumbed to the well-worn review section of the first one, reading in a near-shout, "'An indelible mark on the landscape of contemporary fiction.'" She threw the magazine across the room and watched it flutter to the floor. And in the second publication: "'The boldest new voice of a generation.'" She tore it in half.

She paced the length of her room and back. "Cowards, all of you! You never wanted the truth."

And there was the Lifestyle and Arts page from the Sydney paper. The collection of clippings declared: International Bestseller Lily Davenport Thrills Sydney!—including a photo, a candid shot of Lily at some signing table, head thrown back in laughter or bent in concentration over a book, pen in hand. Each time, without fail, the photo captured a security escort nearby.

Sometimes it was that insufferable woman with the auburn ponytail—Charlie something, what a stupid name!—but often she spotted a blurred silhouette, watchful and always adjacent. Amelia had circled every instance of this Charlie-person's face in red marker, a ring of fire around an intruder.

She sat and clenched her hands, trying to steady them. In the center of the table, she'd set her favorite notebook, battered leather, a relic from a charity shop in Brighton, now swollen with years of printouts and clippings, and annotated so completely that some pages looked more blue than white.

Setting the expensive stationery aside, she opened her notebook and began to write. She filled two pages before stopping. She looked at the evidence—irrefutable, surely—at the blue stains on the pads of her fingers, and felt the satisfaction of a case well built.

She strode to the window and rehearsed the confrontation, this time in a whisper, her mouth close to the glass: "The world will know the truth in the end. You can't hide forever."

Her reflection showed the dark half-moons under her eyes, the wild tangle of her hair, the smudge of ink on her jaw. Better to be a madwoman than invisible.

She nearly smiled, but the old anger surged, more forceful than anything else in the world.

She crossed the room and lay on the bed, the evidence piled beside her—her own notebooks, the pages from the novel, and the newest printouts of critical acclaim—and imagined her triumph. The public, the press, the finale. She would make sure the world understood how the publishers got it all wrong, how she'd been robbed of her chance at fame. This time, she would write the story herself.

And this time, no one would dare call it fiction.

Returning to the desk, she slipped on her favorite gloves; she pulled out a fresh sheet of the creamy stationery, ran her fingers over its surface, and felt a thrill of anticipation. This was it—the last word, the point of no return.

She sat, took a deep breath, uncapped her pen, and watched the tiny drop of ink gather at the nib and flow with the first press to the page. Her hand shook at first, then steadied as she wrote the words she had rehearsed in her head for nearly eight years:

Dear Ms. Davenport,
The time of reckoning approaches.
Here in Rome, the world will see what you have done.
You will not be allowed to forget.
A.

She read it once, twice, delighting in the economy of the threat. No need for theatrics—only the promise of truth. She folded the page with slow, deliberate movements, slid it into the envelope, and sealed it with a dab of water on her gloved fingertip, the way she always did.

Amelia placed the envelope at the apex of her pyramid of evidence, and took a single, measured breath. She closed her eyes and pictured the moment of confrontation: the stage, the audience, the dawning horror on Lily's face as the stolen words were laid bare for all to see.

She opened her eyes. In the mirror above the desk, she allowed herself a victorious smile.

She stood, slipped the letter into her purse. With her

wide-brimmed hat in place, purse slung over her shoulder, she walked down to the street and hailed a cab to take her to the fancier hotel, blocks away.

"Literary thieves must pay," she muttered as she settled into the taxi seat.

Chapter 25

"I'm canceling Rome." Lily greeted us with the stunning announcement at the door to her suite at the Windsor. She wore a midnight-blue robe over flannel pajamas, and the room looked like a post-tornado scene. She stepped aside to admit us.

Louisa's brows arched, silent.

I let the words sit, waiting for the rest to tumble out.

Lily's face was a ruin. "I can't—I can't do it. My publisher will understand. I'll say it's fatigue, or food poisoning, or—" She broke off, made a weak gesture toward the desk, where the threatening notes sat in a messy stack. "I just can't, not with one of these waiting for me every time I open a bloody door."

I stepped forward. "Lily, don't. We've figured out the identity of the stalker."

Her expression froze. "Who?"

"The clues were there in the workshop documents you sent me. We're ninety percent certain it's a former student named Amelia Morris."

"Morris … I vaguely recall…"

Louisa piped up with her recollections of the woman and her attitude in the workshop classes.

Lily took a slow breath as she recalled details. "She gave me a gift, actually. A copy of her manuscript, inscribed with a note that said, 'For the only teacher who never lied to me.' That phrase stuck with me, although I didn't read the manuscript. I put it in the post, along with a note thanking her but saying I couldn't keep the pages. When I tried to email her, the account was dead."

Louisa sipped her tea, eyes bright. "She wanted validation, I think. She needed someone to recognize her as a genuine writer, even if it was only in private. But she couldn't handle anyone else succeeding first."

I looked at Lily, letting her see the weight of my question. "Did you ever feel unsafe around her? Even for a second?"

"No, not at all. Why would she do this now? She barely knew me."

I didn't answer immediately. Instead, I let her ponder the question, let the implications sit there.

Louisa reached out, her fingers gentle on Lily's wrist. "Because you have what she wants. Success, recognition. You moved on, and she stayed behind. Sometimes that's all it takes for old jealousies to raise their head."

"What does she want from me?"

I poured myself a cup of tea, using the time to organize my own thoughts. "To be seen. To be acknowledged.

To have you read and compliment her work, finally. But beyond that—she wants you to know she's there. That you can't outrun her, or the debt she thinks you owe."

She picked up her laptop and sat on the sofa, the computer perched on her knees. Her hands shook as she typed, but her voice was steady. "It'll be in my backups. I saved the workshop folders—in case the student attended a future class."

Louisa hovered nearby, watching.

"There it is," Lily spun the laptop around, the screen showing a PDF labeled "Submission—A. Morris—Session 8 Final."

Louisa leaned in and scanned the first few paragraphs. "I remember this one. She handed out printed copies, but insisted we return them at the end. She said she didn't want her work floating around in the wild."

I moved to the coffee table and read over Lily's shoulder. The story was a tight, twenty-page document, single-spaced and dense with edits in red. The protagonist was a woman abandoned by her lover, who became obsessed with revenge—not through violence, but through a campaign of psychological manipulation. Each page ratcheted up the sense of isolation, of a mind turning in on itself. By the end, the narrator had destroyed not only her enemy, but herself, left standing alone in a city that seemed designed to erase her.

"Is this familiar to you?" I asked, turning to Lily.

She read the first page, her brow furrowing, then flipped to the ending. I watched her face as she scanned the text, saw the color drain out and return gradually. "I don't recall this exact piece, but the notes and comments do look like mine. From what I wrote here in the remarks, the writing was all right, not yet publishable but something that could be shaped up and submitted to one of the short story markets."

"It's ... a revenge story," Louisa said.

"But that's not new. Every third novel these days is a revenge story."

I had her scroll to the very end, checking for author notes. "She left a dedication: 'For anyone who's ever been betrayed. We write so the world will not erase us.'"

"What does that mean?" Louisa demanded. "Is she saying Lily has somehow fulfilled this old grudge, has betrayed Amelia somehow?"

Lily closed the laptop, hugging it to her chest. "My novel isn't about this. None of them are. Not really. There's *a* betrayal in the current one, sure, but the focus is on the aftermath—the recovery, not the obsession. I *never* plagiarized. Never even reread any of my students' work once the workshop was over."

Lily set the computer down, her hands visibly trembling. "What do I do?"

I thought about it. "Gather everything—every note, every email, every scrap of interaction. If she tries anything beyond words, we will involve the police. But, truthfully, I think she's after acknowledgment, not blood."

Louisa nodded. "She wants to be seen."

I stood, stretching the tension from my back. "Don't let her scare you off your own tour."

Lily gave a brittle laugh. "Easier said than done." She pulled her legs up onto the couch, folding into herself. "I don't want to live like this. I don't want to look over my shoulder at all times."

I perched on the coffee table, facing her. "Then don't.

Let us handle it. We'll catch her. You focus on your work, your real life."

She looked so sad that I wanted to hug her. "I thought I could handle it. I've had hecklers, weirdos before. This is different. It makes me feel—" she faltered. "Paranoid. Mad."

Louisa stood and closed the gap. "You're not mad. You're under siege."

"Exactly," Lily said, grateful and desperate all at once. "It's psychological torture. And Rome will be the same—bigger, more public, more press. More opportunities for—" She cut herself off, eyes darting to the envelopes.

I stepped between Lily and the desk, taking her focus. "If you cancel your Rome appearances, Amelia wins."

The words landed with greater force than I intended; Lily blinked at me like I'd thrown cold water on her. I pressed on, softer this time: "If you run, you'll have to keep running. She'll follow you to the next city, or the next book launch, or the next interview. You don't want to spend the rest of your life wondering where she'll pop up."

I let that sit for a few seconds. "And if you cancel, you'll never forgive yourself."

She managed a half-laugh. "That's not fair. I don't care about the tour anymore."

"Not the tour," I said. "Your fans. You didn't get this far by letting them down. Don't start now."

Her hands curled into the fabric of her robe. "You make it sound so simple."

Louisa came up behind her, placing both hands on Lily's shoulders. "It isn't simple. But you're not alone in it. Let us come with you."

She turned to face me, a new spark kindling behind the

exhaustion. "You'd really go? Both of you?"

"Our flight is booked. I can set up the security so there are no surprises, no random envelopes delivered to your room. We'll advise the Rome hotel and the police. I want to set a trap so we catch her this time."

"Thank you." Lily was silent for a long beat. "But what if she's waiting for me in Rome?"

Louisa answered first, laying a hand over Lily's. "Then she's more predictable than we hoped."

I smiled, nodding. "We want her in Rome. We'll be ready this time."

"I've been running scared for weeks," Lily said, her voice quivering. "It feels good to finally fight back."

Louisa poured three cups of hotel tea, distributing them with the solemnity of a pre-battle toast. "To standing your ground," she said.

I raised mine and grinned. "To catching the world's most irritating stalker."

Lily managed a smile, not quite whole but getting there. "To Rome," she said, and clinked her cup against ours. "We're really doing this."

"Yes," I replied. "And we're not alone this time. I've made some calls."

I slugged down the rest of my tea and stood up. "Okay then, it's set. We need to be at the airport by noon, so get your bags packed. I'll schedule a car to pick us up at the Darling and we'll swing by here and get you."

She perked up and began rummaging through the clothing in her closet. Louisa and I left her to it. In the elevator, I leaned against the wall, eyes shut, replaying the scene. The pieces were all there: the stalker, the next venue, the bait. I could only hope and pray the plan came together as I envisioned.

And—if the universe decided to be kind—the long flight wouldn't be too grueling.

Chapter 26

It took me all of five minutes to toss the final items into my bag. Once I'd prepared my carry-on with what I thought I would need for the next thirty-plus hours, I felt a little at loose ends. But there was something from Lily's notes on her workshop students that had stayed with me, the idea that Amelia Morris had eventually submitted one of her stories for publication. Hadn't Lily said something in passing, that she'd heard somewhere that Amelia released a book?

So, while Louisa dithered over what to wear and what to pack, I set my laptop on the desk, opened a browser and typed: "Amelia Morris" + "author."

The first hits were the obvious ones—some confusion with the American vocalist of the same name. I expanded the search string, adding "UK" and "Suffolk" and "Bury

St. Edmunds." Each iteration tightened the results—one mention in a university alumni magazine, a dead link to an abandoned WordPress website, a self-published e-book title that appeared to be a forty-page memoir about being stung by wasps.

I leaned back, rolling my head side to side until the vertebrae in my neck crackled, before I refocused on the screen. This kind of detective work was half muscle memory; you kept clicking, kept refining, until the answers either gave up or you did. I opened a dozen tabs, tiled them across the browser, and let my eyes skim for the odd word that didn't belong.

Three tabs in, a glimmer—a small press in East London, logo like a melting candle, with an "Authors" page that hadn't been updated since Brexit. There she was: A. Morris. No photo, but a two-sentence bio in the brittle, defensive style of someone who wanted the world to see 'serious writer' and not 'desperate wannabe.' I jotted down the publisher, then copied the title of her book: *Further Off*, a slim collection of short stories released to near-complete indifference eight years prior.

Eight years. Right after Lily's fateful workshop.

I clicked over to Amazon.co.uk and found it there. The cover was an amateur affair—cobblestone in grayscale, title superimposed in Times New Roman. It seemed the designer had given up on the concept halfway through and wanted it done. The blurb, presumably written by 'A' herself, promised "unsparing vignettes of longing and isolation."

The only commentary posted was from a blog called The Inkwell Revue, and it was less a review than a polite obituary: "Morris's work is admirably restrained, but perhaps too much so. The best stories gesture at emotion, but don't quite open the door." Aside from that, the book had gathered three reader reviews, all of them two- and three-stars. The book was shown as not currently available.

I cross-referenced the ISBN and searched some other places: WorldCat, Abebooks, and a few others known for their collections of out-of-print books. *Further Off* had never charted, not even warranted a Goodreads rating, and seemed to exist only in the memory of one or two inventory systems still clinging to life in distant corners of the UK.

I wrote a note, flipping to a fresh page in my notepad. Title, publisher, date. The pieces aligned, but I wanted to know the reasons behind this. If A. Morris was Amelia, her fingerprints would be somewhere in the stories. Could there be an obsession with envy, with theft, with being overlooked? Maybe a coded threat or two, if one paid attention.

I searched among the local libraries, but the New South Wales system had not acquired the book, and none of the university libraries had a copy. Which left the back alleys and catacombs of the used book trade. I started with the easy ones—Gleebooks, Berkelouw, Elizabeth's in Newtown. Each site had a search box, and each returned the same: No results found.

But then, on the fifth attempt, a spark: Abbey's Bookshop, here in Sydney, listed a single used copy of *Further Off*. The database had it miscategorized as "travel writing," but there it was—one lone copy, in fair condition, $7.99 Australian.

I checked the time. I had two hours before leaving for the airport, so I called Abbey's, expecting a voicemail, and was rewarded with the sound of an actual human voice, an elderly man by the sound of it. I described the book, saying I'd located it in their searchable database and wanted to be sure the copy of *Further Off* was in stock. He didn't put me on hold, just set the phone down. I could hear shuffling sounds, voices in the distance, and the meow of a cat disconcertingly close to the receiver. After what felt like an hour—actually about ten minutes—he came back and informed me he had the book in his hands.

"Hold it for me, please. I should be there within a half hour." While on hold, I'd searched the address of the shop and estimated I could cover the seven blocks on foot as quickly as waiting for an Uber.

Sure enough, Abbey's Bookshop was right where the search engine said it would be, wedged in a block of cafés and used clothing shops and next to an electronics shop that had not changed its window display in twenty years.

From the outside, Abbey's had a façade that promised order—a tan awning with blue serif lettering, two bright window displays featuring the latest pulp thrillers and Booker Prize hopefuls. Inside, books claimed every surface, in horizontal and diagonal stacks, with the odd sheaf of old magazines thrown in for flavor. The smell of must and paper fiber clung to the air. That it had taken the shopkeeper *only* ten minutes to locate Morris's obscure title actually amazed me.

I ducked under a dangling copy of *Winnie the Pooh* suspended by invisible wire, and made my way to the rear, stepping with care over the geological strata of stock overflow—hardbacks on the bottom, paperbacks near the top, all arranged with the logic of a hoarder who had once intended to alphabetize and then, quite reasonably, surrendered. The sales counter was an island of ancient oak behind which sat a man with skin the color of a good walnut and hair that may have been black decades ago. His glasses hung from a chain, and when he looked up, his eyes were the bright blue of a swimming pool.

"Charlie Parker," I said. "I called about—"

He blinked, nodded, reached into a cubbyhole beneath the register, and fished out a dusty paperback, the same cover I'd seen on the Amazon page. "Ah. The American caller." His voice was like honey. "Morris, is it? *Further Off?*"

"That's the one."

He grimaced, lips pressed into a line. "She did a signing here, you know. Five or six years back. Brought her own tea and everything. One person showed up, probably a sister or cousin or some such. Once that one left, the author sat here for an hour, browsing the shelves and muttering to herself. At the end, she signed six copies, but when I said I'd only take one of them, she left in a strop. Took all the biscuits, too."

He said this with a kind of clinical detachment, as if recalling a childhood incident he'd determined to set aside.

"You have a *very* good memory. Did she seem upset?" I asked.

"Went on a right rant about being wronged by the publishing industry. Said she'd written a masterpiece and no one had the taste to see it." He shrugged. "I've heard worse."

I nodded and let him ring up the book.

The little tome was truly pathetic in the flesh, monotone cover and all. Because of the way it must have been stacked on the shelf, the spine listed slightly forward, giving the book a droop-eyed look.

I thumbed through, careful not to dislodge anything,

and found the author photo on the last page. Amelia Morris was not the sort to flirt with the lens: her dark hair (no gray at the temples yet) was pulled back so tight it made the lines in her forehead pop, and her eyes were two gray chips of quartz. The smile looked carved—posed, without a hint of natural warmth.

I turned a few pages, running my finger along the edges, and saw that several stories had been marked with tiny pencil ticks—by the author herself? Or by the previous owner? The title page was signed all right: "For anyone who's ever been forgotten. A. Morris." The *A* was familiar to me, the rest of the signature hurried and slanted. I wondered who the *anyone* was, and whether she believed it.

The shop manager noticed. "It's a used copy. I hope that's okay."

"Yeah, no problem. I feel lucky to have found it."

He shrugged. "No one else would've called for it, believe me."

I paid with my card, then ventured a question. "Do you recall ... did she talk about anything while she was here?"

The man's eyes flicked to a point above my head. "Hm... Other than what I mentioned ... I think she said she was going to Sydney University. Something about meeting a professor for a possible teaching job. She looked angry about it, though, so I doubt it worked out. I had the impression she's British, didn't live here in Australia."

I thanked him and made my way out, the book tucked flat against my ribs. I felt a weird, twitchy thrill as I strode toward the hotel, the book growing heavier in my hand. It wasn't merely paper; it was evidence. A remnant of a career dream, the echo of a voice so desperate to be heard that it had crossed half the world to haunt a rival. If ghosts existed, I was holding one.

I couldn't wait to see what it had to say, and I had a long flight ahead of me to find out.

Chapter 27

Our airport ride arrived precisely on time, and Louisa and I tucked into the back seat with our baggage in the spacious cargo area. I texted Lily as we were leaving the Darling. She met us in front of the Windsor, dressed for the flight in something burgundy and comfortable, hair looking fresh and precise. I noticed her purposeful body language, that of someone determined not to waste any more time being scared.

When she slid into the seat beside me and saw the book, her smile faltered. "Is that—?"

I nodded. "The only copy in the city, I believe."

She didn't move, but let the title speak for itself. I started with the clerk's story—Amelia's lone signing, the missing crowd, the "right rant" about the failures of taste and the mercenary publishing industry. Lily reached out and picked up the book with the sort of delicacy reserved for unexploded ordnance.

She turned the cover over, read the blurb, and studied the photo on the back page. I observed as she leafed through the pages at her own pace, watching the small tics of her face: curiosity at the first story, recognition at the second, a slow descent into a kind of private grief by the third. When she got to "The Inheritance," she stopped and looked up.

"These were her workshop pieces," she said, almost to herself. "The first drafts. I remember this particular story. The mother dies and the daughter goes mad with the idea that she's been cheated out of something." She looked up at me, blinking fast. "She wrote about loss. Obsession. People who didn't get what they deserved."

"You mean she published them without changing a word?" I asked.

Lily nodded. "Apparently, but that wasn't the point of the workshop. You submit the first draft, but you're supposed to revise, to take feedback and—" She gestured, helpless, at the book. "To make it better. She didn't do the work. She ... she published them as-is."

There was no gloat in her voice, only sadness.

"She wanted to prove something," I said. "To you, or maybe to herself?"

Lily set the book on her lap, opened to the page where her finger had been. "I wrote a note in the margin of this story. Suggested she let the daughter fight back instead of accepting the loss. She didn't like that." Lily traced the line of type. "She said the world never gives back what it takes."

"She was right, in her way."

Lily looked up, the old fire sparking behind the blue.

"But that's the thing, isn't it? You can't narrate your own loss and expect anyone to care about it. You have to shape it, turn it into a universal truth that matters to others. That's what writing is for."

I watched her, taking in the lines of exhaustion and the resolve that lived underneath. "She could have learned so much from you," I said. "If she'd been open to it."

She made a noise—half laugh, half sob. "I feel as though I've let her down. Like I didn't get through to her."

I stared out the window at my last view of the Harbour Bridge, considering. "Her attitude is not your fault. But I think you can give this episode a better ending."

She eyed me sideways. "You have a plan."

"Of course I have a plan."

She smiled, for real this time. "Let's hear it."

I leaned in, lowering my voice to a register that felt suited to espionage. "She thinks you owe her something. She's followed you around the world trying to make you admit it. What if you did?"

Lily frowned. "You want me to … what? Admit plagiarism? Surrender?"

"Not that," I said. "Offer her a meeting. A public one, with witnesses. Tell her you'll acknowledge her—offer to sign her book. Make it about closure, not defeat."

Lily's eyebrows went up. "You think she'll go for it?"

"She's been escalating for months. This is the only ending that makes sense to her. She won't be able to resist."

Lily considered, tapping a slow rhythm against her knee. "And what if she turns violent?"

"We'll be ready. The venue will be full of people. Security, cameras, a few off-duty cops, if I can arrange that. She can't actually do anything without being caught."

Lily picked up the book, flipping to the back where the blurb was a single, meager sentence. "It feels like a trap."

"It is a trap," I said. "And you can walk away from it. If you want to. But it's also a chance to get some help for this disillusioned woman."

For a long moment, she stared at the book, lost in some memory I couldn't follow. Then she closed it, returned it to me, and straightened her spine.

"I'll do it," she said. "But only if you're there. Both of you. I want to end this, but I don't want to do it alone."

I smiled. "You won't have to."

And suddenly we were at the airport, pulling into the departures lane.

I gathered my things, and the three of us trekked toward the doors. We had a stalker to catch, and a ghost to exorcise.

But first, a flight to Rome.

Chapter 28

Rome looked exactly the way I'd imagined: dazzling, impossible, so ancient it made modern problems feel like a blip on the radar. The light was thinning, the sky taking on that deep lavender color of late afternoon. The city did not ease us in. It rose around us all at once. Ancient walls leaned close, scooters filled the air with their whine, and every stone positively reeked of history.

Our car glided past the Colosseum as it glowed from below, its arches lit like a living thing, resting between battles rather than an ancient ruin.

The car, arranged by Lily's publishing team, dropped us in a little piazza off the Corso Vittorio, where everything glowed under a setting sun that turned the yellow stone of the buildings into gold. Even this late in the day, the temperature was hovering around eighty—we'd definitely left behind the rainy chill of late winter in Australia. I found myself immediately peeling off layers of clothing.

Across the way, cafés spilled onto the sidewalks, chairs scraping, glasses chiming, voices layered in a language I could not understand, but I somehow caught the meaning. The air smelled of espresso, warm bread, and a long, noisy history.

"This is our new hotel." Lily was first out of the car. She scanned the block with wide eyes that reminded me we already had an adversary in this city.

This was another convenience added by the publisher behind the book tour, a last-minute switch of hotels to throw our predator off the scent.

Louisa followed, pulling a powder-blue suitcase, her shoes absolutely not made for cobblestones. I started to settle the fare with the driver—who waved away the money, saying the charges were taken care of—and then I took a full sweep of the street before letting myself believe we'd actually arrived.

The hotel didn't stand out, which was the point. Some converted palazzo, heavy on climbing vines and windows, and short on signage, three steps up from street level and flanked by cafés that advertised American breakfast.

What stood out: the two men in street clothes posted near the entrance, one holding a phone he wasn't using, the other pretending to check his watch at fifteen-second intervals. To their right, a carabinieri in full uniform, pretending to write a parking ticket for a car thirty feet away. The effect was less *danger* than *VIP in residence*, and I wondered if that was a good idea.

Lily hesitated at the foot of the steps, but I verified that the guards had been arranged at our request. I guided us up to the entrance, where a doorman intercepted us with the practiced ease of someone who could size up a guest before the revolving door made a full rotation.

"Welcome, Signora, *benvenuta*," he said, bowing enough to signal his deference. He switched to English. "The desk is right inside. May I help with your bags?"

I shook my head, and so did Lily, so he took Louisa's bag and seamlessly opened the inner door. The lobby was all cool marble and antique-styled chairs, with a long glass-topped desk staffed by a trio of women who could have passed as runway models on their day off. The desk manager looked up, fixed on Lily, and greeted her by name.

"Ms. Davenport. Welcome to the Hotel Tevere. We've been expecting you.," She said it with the perfect mixture of warmth and professional distance. "You're in the executive suite, as requested. For security, we've restricted all other guests from your floor and implemented a 24-hour surveillance schedule. If you have any preferences for housekeeping or room service timing, please inform us and we'll adjust accordingly."

Lily nodded, but said nothing.

The manager smiled, slid a registration form across the glass, and requested our passports. "If you could sign here, please." Lily scrawled her initials so quickly that the writing was completely unlike the autographs in her books.

Louisa was taking in the classical décor in the lobby, the little niches in the corridors. "Do you have ghosts on the premises?"

The manager smiled politely, happy to play along. "Only the friendly ones, Signora."

Returning our passports, the manager reached under the desk for three keycards and turned to Lily. "There is also a note for you, Ms. Davenport."

Lily visibly flinched away from the outstretched envelope until she realized the paper was ordinary office white, nothing like the others. Nonetheless, she stepped aside and let me take the message from the other woman.

I ripped open the envelope and studied the single page inside. "It's from the local police liaison, an Inspector Antonia Ricci. She requests a brief meeting tomorrow at one o'clock, here in the hotel conference room, to go over procedures for your event."

Lily turned toward the desk manager. "Thank you. Can you make sure I'm not disturbed until then?"

"Of course," the woman said. "We have instructed all staff to minimize contact, and no visitors will be told of your presence."

We took the lift—mirrored, the kind that made every flaw in your posture stand out—and rode in mutual silence up to the fourth floor. The hallway was empty, the carpet so new it had the creases from installation. Our suite was at the end, an adjoining pair of rooms and a living area with double doors. By mutual agreement, Louisa and I would take the smaller one, with twin beds; Lily would have the other.

Lily went straight to the window and pulled the curtain aside. The dome of St. Peter's, illuminated against the darkening sky, hovered in the distance. She pressed her hand to the glass and breathed, slow and shallow.

Louisa dumped her bag on one of the twin beds, while I immediately began a tour of the room's boundaries, checking windows, bathrooms, balcony, every door and closet. It all checked out, secure and tight.

Lily had not moved from the window. "You think she'll

come here?" she asked, not turning around.

I shook my head. "No. She wants the audience. She wants you scared, but she wants you to show up. For her, Rome is the main event."

Louisa hovered in the doorway to the balcony, voice brisk. "She's right, darling. If this woman has followed you from London to Sydney, she's not going to stop. But if we do this by the book—if we're careful—she'll trip herself up."

Lily closed her eyes. "I want it to be over."

I stepped up beside her, kept my hands in my pockets, and watched the street four stories below. "It will be. But we have to play it through. At least this time, I think we'll have some backup."

She nodded, finally, and backed away from the glass. I stood there, savoring a quiet moment. Night made Rome intimate. Streetlamps cast a soft golden light along cobblestones polished by centuries of footfalls. Below our window sat a small piazza where a fountain murmured to itself, water sliding over marble worn smooth as skin.

Cafés bustled; the dinner hour here was only beginning. Laundry fluttered between buildings a block away. The feeling was as if emperors and saints and ordinary Romans were out there, to see how I was taking it all in. I turned to the others and asked if anyone was hungry.

But our internal clocks were a mess, and we all wanted sleep more than food. We unpacked in silence, each of us working through the motions of normal life and our separate thoughts. I charged my phone and went through my email, deleting at least three-quarters of the messages.

One that I did read was from the book tour coordinator, and I skimmed the itinerary for Lily's big event, day after tomorrow at the Biblioteca Nazionale: arrival at 11:30, green room at 11:45, public reading at noon, followed by a two-hour signing with VIP reception after. The security detail would meet us in our hotel lobby at eleven, escort us to the venue, and stay with us until we were safely on our way back.

I shut down my laptop, suddenly fatigued to the bone, practically asleep before I peeled off my clothes and fell into bed.

Chapter 29

The problem with an early bedtime is that it leads to an early awakening. In my case, my body was telling me it was midday, although it was barely after two a.m. here in Rome. I lay in bed as long as I could, but I was worried that my tossing and turning would wake Louisa. I got up, pulled on my robe, gathered my notebook and a novel I'd been trying to read for over a week, and tiptoed from our bedroom to the suite's living room.

The beverage bar in the corner provided a variety of coffees and teas, but I opted for the least potent, a chamomile. Scrolling through my phone, looking nostalgically at what the weather might be at home, I realized it was close to mid-morning in New Mexico, the perfect time to give Drake a call.

"So, Rome, huh?" he teased, by way of greeting.

"You saw my text about our arrival, I guess. What a journey this has been, and I'm so eager to see you again." I heard the dog whine in the background, which brought tears to my eyes. "And Freckles. I miss you both."

We exchanged updates, something we'd only managed every fourth or fifth day since I'd left home. While he was filling me in on an upcoming Forest Service job, I caught myself yawning. He heard it too. We said a bunch of mushy stuff, mainly about how good it would feel to be together, before we ended the call. I sipped my cooled chamomile and picked up my notebook.

Within a half hour, I'd reread all my case notes and failed to complete a chapter in the novel before I'd drifted off to sleep. My dozing thought was how glad I was that we had a full day to return to routine before tackling the tension of Lily's public appearance.

Morning arrived gently, and I felt a hand brush my shoulder to wake me. Louisa whispered, "I'm going out for a walk. Want to come?"

Well, of *course* I did. It was my first time in Rome, and I really didn't want to spend all of it dominated by the ongoing situation with our author friend. I wiped grains of sleep from my eyes and stumbled into the bedroom to get dressed. By the time I emerged, Louisa had written a note to Lily, suggesting she text one of us when she woke up. We could bring breakfast.

Out on the street, the light was different, pale, revealing every chip and crack and making them beautiful instead of tired. We crossed the Tiber as the river slid past, green and slow, reflecting bridges that seemed to float. I'd forgotten what a rich and varied life my aunt had led. She was the free spirit, the wild child, apparently, compared to my father, and she had wasted no time seeing the world during her youth.

She set out now with a purpose, which was to show me the old haunts where she had hung out fifty years ago.

At the Pantheon, sunlight poured through the oculus and struck the floor like a spotlight meant for the gods, and for a moment I forgot to move. Nearby, Piazza Navona was buzzing. We strolled its length before heading toward the Trevi Fountain, which was much more cramped than I'd expected. Tourists were gathering, coins flashing briefly before vanishing into water and wishes.

Louisa's gaze grew soft. "What stayed with me most about this city was not any single monument, grand as they are, but the way Rome layers itself. There are deeply buried secrets here, things we British can barely conceive, and Americans…"

"We have no clue. I know." I savored the aroma of coffee in the air.

"I didn't mean to say it exactly that way," she said with a laugh, "but two-hundred-fifty years is quite young."

My phone chimed, a text bringing me back to the twenty-first century. "Lily says she's content to have a small room service breakfast and stay in. 'Have fun on your adventures!' is how she ends the message."

Louisa brightened. "In that case, I have the perfect thing. We'll tuck on over to where the best pastry shop in all of Rome happens to be—it's only a block away. A bag of *cornetto*, assorted flavors, and we'll get an espresso to go with them. And before the temperature gets too hot, we can sit beside the fountain to eat."

"Sounds like a plan." I'd been wondering how my aunt's fair English skin would handle the intense August sun here.

As we sipped our coffee and nibbled pastry, morning bells chimed over the traffic. A woman swept her stoop beneath a two-thousand-year-old arch. Vines climbed walls older than my entire country. I felt small and strangely comforted by it, as if the city were telling me that time was vast, beauty was persistent, and I was lucky to be allowed, briefly, to be part of the story.

Once we finished eating, we could easily grab a taxi and spend the part of the morning at a gallery or museum before our date with the police.

* * *

At one p.m., the desk manager called to announce the arrival of our police liaison: Inspector Antonia Ricci. Lily said we would meet her in the hotel conference room in ten minutes. I went to the adjoining room to find Louisa laying out clothing on her bed.

She looked up, caught my eye, and said, "You're going to need a nap, darling. No one solves anything after only three hours' sleep."

"Too wired," I said. "You?"

She laughed. "Adapting myself to this time zone. But not opposed to an afternoon lie-down." She held up two shirts. "For tomorrow, the turquoise or the white?"

"For the book event, I'd go with the turquoise," I said.

I left her and found Lily standing near the window, her face pale but composed.

"What's the plan?" she asked.

"Ricci is here, getting set up in the conference room. We'll walk through the event logistics, see what she advises. We'll probably stay low-key until tomorrow."

She nodded. "What if Amelia doesn't show?"

"She'll show," I said. "People like this don't want to miss their own climactic moment."

Lily laughed—only once, but a real laugh. "You're good at this, you know."

"We all have our talents."

I made sure Louisa had her hotel key, picked up my case file, and walked with Lily to the conference room on the mezzanine level. The door was open, and Ricci was waiting—a woman of about fifty, hair pulled into a tight black twist, eyes that took in everything. She wore a plain suit and flat shoes, and her handshake was brisk, almost American.

"You are Ms. Parker?" she said. The accent was thick but her English was perfect.

"Yes," I said, and introduced Lily as my client.

She motioned us to the table, where three folders and a bottle of water waited. "We will be brief," she said. "Mainly to cover the layout of the Biblioteca, to be sure everyone knows their places."

Ricci opened a folder and produced a diagram and photos of the event venue—a building of starkly modern appearance compared to most of what I'd seen in Rome. "The library, of course, is open to the public, but the room where the event is to be held will be restricted to those holding tickets. We will have plainclothes officers at each entrance to the room. The media will be controlled, and all bags searched."

She unfolded the venue map—a scaled printout of the Biblioteca Nazionale's ground floor. "There are several entrances. Main doors are here, side entrances for staff, loading dock is at the rear. The signing event is in this chamber—" she pointed "—but there's a media room upstairs and a café on the mezzanine. We cannot possibly cover every square meter, nor can we prevent a patron from entering the building."

Lily spoke up. "My publisher tells me at least two hundred tickets were issued, with a dozen press and another ten VIPs on the guest list."

Ricci nodded, pointed with her pen. "We will have four plainclothes officers on the floor. One at each entrance, two in the crowd. There are baggage scanners at the main doors. Side and rear entrances will be manned. There will be a medical team staged in the basement, in case of a stampede or incident."

"Media badges?" I asked.

"All will be checked against the register. Anyone with a bag or equipment goes through a search. No exceptions." She smiled thinly. "We do not want a repeat of Palermo."

I didn't ask about Palermo, not wanting to get sidetracked. "What about surveillance? Cameras?"

Ricci nodded. "There are cameras in the main public areas, and we will monitor in real time from the control room."

I hesitated. "If Amelia Morris approaches, do you have authority to detain her?"

"We can detain anyone who poses a disruption. If she tries to enter with fake credentials, or if she brings something dangerous, she will be in custody before she sees the stage."

We all stared at the layout of the building, each with our own thoughts.

The inspector looked at me. "Your role?"

"I plan to stay close, within sight of Ms. Davenport at

all times, as will another member of our party."

Ricci liked that answer. "Good. If you have concerns, you bring them to me directly. We will be in communication throughout the event. Otherwise, we will keep this quiet. No drama, yes?"

"No drama," Lily echoed, but I heard the doubt. "Amelia could be disguised, couldn't she?"

"She could," I said. "But we'll know her."

"Ms. Parker," Ricci said, "this reminds me ... you have a case file to share?"

I laid out the evidence in ascending order of drama: the five notes and the envelopes, the printout of the stationery provenance, and finally the grid of annotated workshop rosters and manuscript excerpts.

Ricci pulled out a pair of small reading glasses, and the act of donning them somehow doubled her authority. She worked her way through the evidence, eyes darting between the actual threat notes and the report I'd prepared overnight. When she got to the printout from the stationer in Notting Hill and copy of the purchase invoice, she grunted—a short, approving sound.

"You are very organized," she said.

"I try," I replied.

"You believe this connects the sender to London?"

"She was living there when the campaign started," I said, tracing the route of the book tour. "We think she's using Rome as the final stage. The pattern escalates with the tone of each successive message."

I flipped to the next document: the workshop group photo, with Amelia Morris circled in red. I kept the author photo of Amelia from the jacket of her book for the big reveal at the end. "The photos are about eight years old.

Sorry, I have nothing more recent that shows her face. She's been diligent about avoiding cameras."

Ricci nodded. "Tell me about your client's connection?"

"Amelia attended a writing workshop with Lily. Since then, she's published one unsuccessful book and spent years tracking Lily's career. She's obsessed, but we have no idea when she will cross the line from written threats to physical violence."

Ricci sat back, folding her hands. "But she has not made a direct threat. Only ... implication."

"Correct," I said. "But her last note—" I slid it forward— "was increasingly aggressive. She went directly to Ms. Davenport's hotel room. We believe she's here and she's watching."

Ricci studied the note and the photo on the book cover, lips pursed. "I can have this photograph enlarged and distributed to our men at the venue."

I nodded, glad to know this. "Louisa and Lily may be the only ones who will recognize Amelia immediately. The photo is old. She has attended the author's other events, often wearing a loose coat and large hat. A coat would be noticed immediately here, in this warm weather, but she's likely to use some type of disguise."

Ricci considered. "You will be at the foot of the stage, left side. Security will listen to you. If you see her, you make a sign—something small, yes?"

I made a mental note to coordinate with Louisa. "Yes. If she's there, we'll spot her."

The inspector closed the file and slipped the reading glasses into her pocket. "You are more thorough than most of my detectives," she said, "but you are still American. You like to control every detail. Sometimes, it is not possible."

I smiled, a little sheepish. "I understand. And I do know that control is a myth, but it makes people feel better."

She pulled Amelia's book and the group photo that included her image and handed my case file back to me. "We will do what we can. But be ready for anything. In Rome, the show is always bigger than you expect."

It sounded like the type of statement a local cop would make. I took the folder, shouldering the implied warning. "Thank you, Inspector."

"If it goes badly, do not try to be a hero. Let my people handle it."

I promised her, but down inside I knew I lied—this Amelia character had eluded me for more than a week. I would do whatever it took. Ricci closed the folder and stood. "Then we are done." We exchanged phone numbers, ready to call or text each other as things developed.

Lily and I walked toward the suite together. I scanned the halls, but nothing moved except the squeaky wheels of a maid's cart. When we got inside, Louisa had ordered a tray of prosciutto and hard cheese—her version of comfort food—and rotated through her arsenal of teas. She had laid out the snacks, no doubt purchased from some impressive little shop she knew about, and was working through a crossword puzzle in Italian, pen tapping the page with impatience.

"Well?" she asked.

"Tomorrow, we go to war," I said. "Tonight, we eat cheese and pretend we're merely tourists."

Louisa grinned. "That I can do." And for a minute, the world was normal.

Chapter 30

She walked up to the check-in desk, the note held in one gloved hand. Smile? Or maintain a businesslike detachment? She debated as she waited for the clerk to turn around. Businesslike, it would be. Putting on an aloof expression, she extended the cream-colored envelope to the young man. He reached for it.

"*Per un ospite?*"

At her blank look, he switched to English. "Is this for one of our guests?"

"Yes, Ms. Lily Davenport." Really, the man couldn't simply look at the name on the envelope?

He set the envelope down and turned to his computer terminal, tapping keys. "I'm afraid we have no one by that name staying with us."

Amelia's mind raced. "Is there a Charlie Parker? Or

someone from Crown Publishing?"

He was only willing to go so far to be helpful. "I am sorry, Signora."

Amelia snatched up the note and backed away. At every other hotel on the tour, Lily had registered under her own name. Had she canceled this leg of her trip?

She retreated to a corner of the lobby and dropped onto a chair upholstered in burgundy stripes. Pulling out her phone, she rechecked the book signing venue, the Biblioteca Nazionale's website listed the appearance of 'British bestselling author, Lily Davenport' as today's key event.

So, her nemesis had switched hotels at the last minute. Was there any possibility she'd learned that Amelia was staying here herself?

No matter. She would attend the event, for which she'd obtained her ticket weeks ago, and when the Q&A period began, she would join the queue to deliver both the written note and to say her piece. With a smile on her face, she walked to the lift and rode to the third floor, ready to begin her preparations for what might be the most important day of her life.

Chapter 31

We were all stirring before the sky was fully light. Time zone differences, a big day ahead of us, nerves—whatever the reasons, we found ourselves milling about well before most Romans. Louisa suggested a long walk, but I could tell Lily didn't really have the urge to get outside. We agreed that a big breakfast would fortify us, so rather than going with the light, sweet preference of most Italians, we placed an order with room service for the full English.

Lily retreated to her bedroom when the knock came at the door. I was the one to ascertain that the delivery was legit, and once the table was set up in our living room, we gathered. I had to admit that the eggs, sausages, beans, tomatoes and toast were more satisfying to me than a pastry, knowing I had a pretty full day ahead. We were laying our napkins aside when the conversation turned to the topic on everyone's mind.

"I'll be fine," Lily said, before anyone asked. "I think I have a good feel for the venue and what's expected of me."

I looked at her. *She's the bravest of all of us, keeping her cool up on that stage.*

"Reviewing the plan, we'll leave the hotel around eleven," I said. "No last-minute changes. No unexpected guests. If anything feels dangerous, we abort."

Louisa exhaled, a soft whuff of air. "Understood."

I turned in my chair, facing Lily. "You're the target, but you're also the bait. Amelia needs you to see her. It's what she really wants."

Lily met my gaze; she looked curious rather than scared. "What happens after?"

I didn't know, but I said, "We'll figure it out. Together." Today, everything would come to a head. I hoped we were ready for it.

We each busied ourselves with a lot of nothing for an hour or so. Outside, the city ticked toward mid-morning, and the air shimmered with the heat.

Lily paced the perimeter of the living area, book in hand, reading aloud in a voice that wobbled at the edges but never quite broke. She'd decided to read a different passage than at the previous signings. She stopped occasionally to mark a page with a sticky flag or jot a reminder before circling to the sofa to start over.

Each time she hit the page with the line—her line, but the one she was sure Amelia had claimed as her own—she'd pause, fingers tightening on the book's spine, as if by sheer force of grip she could rewrite the history of this whole drama. I watched her, wanting to say something helpful but knowing that the ritual of rehearsing her lines mattered more than any comfort I could give. I supposed writers had their superstitions.

Louisa, meanwhile, was studying Lily's two possible outfits—a white silk blouse and the notorious red one—and was holding up the latter. "It'll catch the light," Louisa said, half to herself. "No one will be able to miss you in this. You'll look like a lighthouse on the podium."

Lily made a noncommittal noise, eyes on her marked-up page. "I wasn't thinking I'd be a target when I packed for this trip. But I suppose it's too late for that."

Louisa shrugged, gave a tiny smile. "Better to be a well-dressed one, I say."

I crossed to the balcony, checked the sight lines from the glass, and calculated the various angles someone could use to view the room from the street. Wondering where in this city Amelia Morris was presently, I realized that if she knew which were our windows and wanted to get a look, she'd have to do it from the scaffolding of a half-renovated church two buildings over, or from the café across the square—a possibility. I scanned the windows, balconies, and sidewalks across the way, looking for any sign of a watcher—I saw none.

When I came in, Lily had moved to the window and was staring at St. Peter's, the dome gleaming in the sun. She ran her fingertip up and down the glass, like she was tracing the city into memory.

"You ready?" I asked softly.

She didn't look at me, but I heard her exhale. "I thought I would be," she said. "But every time I practice, I hear her voice under mine. Like she's standing behind me, reading the lines as I say them. What if I actually did borrow something of hers?"

"We reviewed all your notes, Lily. I didn't see anything close enough in her work to make me think she has any legitimate claim. Do you? Think so?"

Louisa came over and held out a cup of tea. "That's the thing about the ghosts of our past, darling. You can only hear them if you're afraid."

Lily laughed, a brittle sound. "So, if I pretend not to care, she'll go away?"

Louisa grinned. "No. But it'll piss her off."

That brought a smile, brief but real. I walked over and joined them at the window.

"We'll be right beside you the whole time," I said. "She'll have to get through us first."

Lily set her book on the sill and turned. "What if she tries to talk to me? What if she tries to make me confess to stealing her work, or creates some awful scene?"

I looked at her, then at Louisa, who nodded encouragement.

"You let her talk," I said. "You let her say whatever she needs to. If she puts you on the spot, ask her to read the portions from her own work and yours. The burden of proof is on her, and we know she can't do it. But most of all, you don't let her define you. That's the part she didn't understand. You get to decide how this ends."

Lily considered and picked up her book. "I won't let her win," she said. "Even if she rips off her dress and dances around the library naked for the attention she so craves."

Louisa cackled. "Please let her try. That would make all of this worthwhile."

I laughed, the tension unspooling a little, and for that little while we were three women in a beautiful city.

"To surviving the lunatics," Louisa toasted, raising her tea mug.

Lily clinked her mug against ours. "To telling your own story."

Somewhere in the distance, a bell tolled, and the sound blended with the morning sounds of the city, echoing like a promise. Our ride would be here in an hour.

Chapter 32

It was nearly time.

Amelia ran through her mental checklist once more: disguise, evidence, escape route, timing. She'd decided on some important changes this time and wanted to assure everything went smoothly. She folded a fifty-euro note around her hotel keycard ("in case," she whispered, as if money could be a talisman) and slipped them into the pocket of her slacks. She checked the window, and this time let her gaze linger on the city below.

Rome was a bustling city, the streets filling with traffic, the morning's damp heat gathering itself for the day. She watched the street for a full five minutes, noting the uniforms, the delivery vans, the comings and goings around the front entry. The regularity of it soothed her; this was a rhythm she could exploit.

Turning back to the bed, she ran her hand over the wig, the gloves, the evidence that would make her case against the criminal acts of Lily Davenport. She fitted her notebook full of evidence into her purse, satisfied that it went inside without a bulge. It occurred to her that bags might be searched at the library, so she removed the other item. She could tuck that somewhere on her person. She flexed her fingers. Steady. In control.

She picked up the wig and walked into the adjoining bathroom, pinning her own hair up and slipping the highlighted blonde hair in place. Her makeup bag provided the other tools—foundation a shade rosier than her own skin, blusher in a soft peach, lip gloss designed to make her appear younger, fresher. She smiled at the result.

Amelia had no idea whether the Parker woman had come up with a photo of her; somewhere in Sydney she might have snapped one. But this—the image in the mirror—was the new version. It would take an expert eye to see the old Amelia in a crowded room. As a final touch, she added a pair of non-prescription glasses.

She returned to the bedroom and sat on the side of the bed, the wig perfectly in place, the glasses slightly askew in the manner of an absent-minded academic. She rehearsed her lines once again, pitching her voice softer, slower, more self-effacing. She listened, analyzing her tone of voice, the words she'd say when she stood up and accused the thief.

Amelia allowed herself a single moment to think about the confrontation—how Lily's face would register first confusion, then terror, and finally, recognition. She savored the imagined crack in the perfect public mask, the moment when the *real* Lily would surface, exposed as a fraud in the moments before she broke down and cried out her apologies.

She'd planned this encounter carefully for years. She wanted to be acknowledged for her work. She wanted the world to know what had been taken from her.

She stood, squared her shoulders, and walked to the mirror. Wearing a fitted pantsuit and burgundy lace blouse, the woman who stared at her was not Amelia Morris; gone were the big hat and long, flowing coat. She smiled, relaxed it, and practiced an expression of mild curiosity. She tried out a few voices, settling on one: breathy, uncertain, unthreatening.

"Today, everyone will know the truth about Lily Davenport," she whispered to her reflection.

The mirror did not answer.

Chapter 33

The Biblioteca Nazionale looked more like a modern-day apartment building than a resemblance to the other architecture in Rome. But the gardens surrounding it were beautifully trimmed and softened the effect of the steel and glass edifice. Since we were traveling with the private security detail I'd arranged ahead of time, we would be in two vehicles. I arrived in the first, well over an hour before Lily's signing.

The front entrance was cordoned by a velvet rope and a pair of temporary luggage scanners, both manned by bored-looking employees who'd clearly drawn the short straw for Sunday overtime. Inside, the main desk was attended by an efficient-looking woman who could probably tell you what aisle and what shelf contained any book, in any language, you wanted to locate.

I found the main reading chamber—where the reading and Q&A would unfold—had been prepped into a kind of amphitheater. Rows of chairs fanned out from a small, raised dais, and every item in the room stood precisely in its place. There were banners with Lily's face (a soft smile on her features), and at the back, a table for book sales stacked with hardcovers in both English and Italian. I paused at the entrance to send Inspector Ricci a text to let her know of my arrival before I began my circuit.

With the layout of the facility firmly in my mind, I located the entrances and exits where I knew them to be. Ricci was present with her team, the promised plainclothes officers, and she gave me a small nod. The officers spread out, a couple of them taking up positions near the exits, two others mingling with the people who were trickling in through the doors, consulting their tickets, and looking for their seats.

Louisa walked in, which told me that Lily was safely in the green room—or likely a cubicle that had been designated as such—with her publisher escorts and whoever had been chosen to emcee the event and introduce her. My aunt took her seat in the front row, and the high flush in her cheeks told me she was ready to leap into action if necessary.

I stepped over and bent down to say hello.

"I'm saving you this seat," she said, patting the jacket she'd laid across the adjacent chair.

"Thanks. I'm going to wander, keep my eyes on things. I saw Ricci and her team."

"Oh, good. Glad that part of it came together." She squeezed my hand when I reached to pat her shoulder.

It took a good thirty minutes for the large room to fill, and in all that time I didn't see one long, navy coat or a wide-brimmed hat. Disappointing, yes. Surprising, no.

As things settled, the house lights blinked and dimmed a little. Stage lights came on and the crowd automatically hushed. A woman in a chic black dress entered from the right and took the podium. From my position to the left of the stage, I could see Lily waiting in the wings with a copy of her book tucked in her arms, her eyes gently closing as she took a deep breath.

I tuned out most of the introduction, which began with, "A bestselling author who needs no introduction …" The message was repeated in both English and Italian. My eyes were on the crowd, making me wish the house lights weren't *quite* so dim. And then, "We are pleased to welcome British author *Lily Davenport*."

As Lily walked on stage, the applause wasn't quite rock-star level, but close. She smiled and waved to the audience, an amazing face of calm, considering what I knew she'd been through. She took her place behind the podium and opened her book to the marked page, fingers curled lightly around the edge, as the house lights receded further and the spotlight made her the star of the room. The effect was to blur everything else—audience, backdrop, the oversized author photo on the screen behind her.

She greeted the audience in Italian, then reverted to English, apologizing for her accent and instantly ingratiating herself with everyone in the place.

I had staked out the aisle by the emergency exit, and I saw Inspector Ricci at the rear of the room. The two other officers feigned indifference, but I'd seen the discreet bulge of service weapons under their jackets.

Lily began with a short talk on process—the endless drafts, the jokes about mainlining caffeine, the myth that writers *channel* rather than grind away at their keyboards.

She acknowledged, with modesty, that her years of teaching had finally paid off. There was polite laughter, the kind that sounds like applause.

She moved into her reading, a selection from the new book. I'd heard her practicing it, but now the words contained a current: the sharp little betrayals, the offhand cruelty of families, the hunger for approval that hovered over the characters. For a few minutes, the only sound in the room was her voice, threading the silence with a spell so fine even Ricci's officers looked up from their phones to listen.

That's when the perimeter collapsed.

Chapter 34

The whole thing was too much. Amelia tried breathing through it, something her therapist had recommended when her temper flared. Think of positive things. She could take pride in the fact that she'd arrived without being spotted, and her bag was scanned without incident at the main entry. She had immediately spotted the Parker woman, lingering at the edges of the aisles, as if she actually belonged here.

And there, in the front row, was Louisa Parker. The connection became clear all at once. Louisa from the writing workshop. How dare she come here and bring this busybody relative of hers to spoil Amelia's own moment of vengeance? How could she!

From the moment Lily Davenport took the stage, Amelia had to entwine her fingers to keep them from shaking. They ached as Lily made her silly, self-deprecating remarks; her knuckles cracked as the author began reading.

Then, one passage from the book was the final straw. Amelia felt a white-hot surge of anger as the words came over the PA system, burning their way into her brain.

Gone was her organized plan to stand and carefully confront the woman who had ruined her life.

Chapter 35

We caught only a small noise at first—a chair scraping hard against the floor, followed by the slap of shoes that were not made for running. A murmur started on the left, picked up by the people who turned first. The woman cut through the row, a sudden, animal lunge.

I saw the initial confusion on the faces in the audience—was she ill, in pain, upset enough to warrant a quick escape from the room? But I spotted the gleam of vengeance in her eyes, the single-minded focus on the podium at the front. She didn't look like the woman I'd chased through the woods, but—

Then I saw the hair—a blonde wig, poorly perched and slipping at the crown, framing a face I barely recognized from the one old photo and the hurried glimpses I'd caught in recent days.

Amelia Morris, live and in the flesh.

She carried something clutched to her chest—a sheaf of pages or a notebook? The wig bounced with each step, and beneath it her face revealed the tension of nerves, jaw clenched, eyes wide and frantic. Two security men saw her, but too late. By the time they moved, she was at the foot of the stage, already howling her first accusation.

"She's a fraud!" The voice fractured on the high notes, but the echo carried to the last row. "This woman stole my words—my ideas, my life's work!"

For a second, the entire hall went dead silent.

Lily froze. The blood drained so quickly from her cheeks I thought she might pass out, but her hands remained on the podium. The microphone, still live, picked up every tremor in her breathing.

Amelia scrambled up the steps, scattering a few manuscript pages that fluttered across the risers and landed at Lily's feet. She seized the microphone with both hands and wrenched it toward herself, her eyes fixed on Lily like an angry predator. Lily took two steps back, her eyes searching the room for help.

"Tell them!" Amelia shrieked, and her expression flashed, as naked as any I'd ever seen. "Tell them how you took my story—the one about betrayal, about being erased, about watching yourself disappear!"

A shudder ran through the crowd, that delicious, frisson of terror that we might all be living in someone else's novel. A good number of them probably wondered if this was all part of the show, an enactment of a scene or some such.

I dashed toward the melee, but saw Ricci in motion, angling for the side steps to the stage. Two plainclothes from the local crew flanked the aisle, hands to their jackets, but hesitant: there was no weapon yet, no explicit threat, just the raw, vicious accusation finally set loose.

Lily opened her mouth, tried to speak, but nothing came out but the shallow, arrhythmic gasping of a person who is temporarily speechless. She'd told me she was prepared for a face-to-face confrontation, but I knew she hadn't dreamed it would go this way.

The program director, the woman in the black dress, darted forward to intervene, but Amelia shoved her with surprising force. She held the microphone and turned toward the room, wild-eyed, the fake blonde hair fully askew.

"Look at the dates!" she screamed toward the audience. "Look at the work! She was my teacher—I trusted her! She took my story and sold it and left me nothing!"

Each word landed like a fist.

Behind me, someone gasped—maybe Louisa, maybe the entire front row. The crowd dissolved into a surge of whispers, and I could tell they were considering whether the charge could possibly be true.

Amelia brandished the manuscript at Lily, shoving it under her nose. "Admit it!" she said. "Admit what you did! Tell them how you stole my work and left me behind!"

By now the officers had mounted the stage, but no one wanted to be the first to lay hands on a woman in the throes of what might—possibly—be justice. Lily shrank away, white-faced, her eyes darting from Amelia's face to the sea of expectant faces in the audience.

For a single, endless second, all three—the accuser, the accused, the observer—hung motionless. Manuscript pages dropped to the floor as her right hand reached into the waistband of her black slacks.

It took a moment to realize she'd drawn a knife.

I broke away first, vaulting onto the stage and landing in front of the podium. I planted myself between Lily and Amelia, hands up, voice low and calm, the way you talk a ledge-jumper back into the world.

"Enough," I said, but the word sounded more like a prayer than an order.

Amelia locked eyes with me, and I felt as though I saw through her—the pain, the history, the bottomless hunger to be recognized—even if only as the villain in someone else's story.

"Lily Davenport will never admit it," she said, voice dropping to a whisper. "But you know I'm right."

I didn't answer. Arguing by supplying facts and examples rarely works to change a fanatic's mind.

The loose manuscript pages, caught by the air conditioning, drifted across the stage like autumn leaves. The crowd did not breathe. Every molecule of air had been sucked from the room. All eyes followed the accusatory orbit of Amelia Morris, who circled the podium with her knife raised, as if this were the kill-or-be-killed moment. Out in the audience, I glimpsed multiple phones raised, cameras catching the unfolding drama.

Lily, for her part, staggered backward one full step. For an instant, I feared she'd collapse, that she might succumb to one of those vaporous fainting spells that only happens to famous women in novels. But she held, teeth clenched, eyes fixed on the chaos in front of her. The program director took her arm, ready to hustle her off the stage.

I caught Ricci's attention and gave the signal; her people responded immediately. From stage left, two plainclothes officers advanced with hands spread wide, voices low and disarming. "Please, calm down … let us help…"

But Amelia wasn't there to be helped. Her left hand was full of the tattered, fluttering manuscript, and she held it high over her head as a proclamation, the way prophets once held stone tablets.

"She's lying!" Amelia shrieked, voice gone ragged and raw. "Look at the dates—look at the bloody handwriting! Every story, every scene—she took them from me!"

She hurled the handful of pages into the air, a blizzard of accusations. The crowd stayed frozen in their seats. I could feel the collective pulse of two hundred hearts pounding in unison, a primal warning of a predator—or the modern equivalent, the cliffhanger ending on a reality show.

Behind the first wave of security, a uniformed officer posted at the main exit unsnapped the leather loop on his sidearm holster. Another moved to block the VIP corridor, radio raised to his lips as he mumbled rapid-fire Italian. I saw Louisa, behind the commotion, standing absolutely frozen, her eyes locked on me with matronly, protective intensity.

Lily tried to speak. "This isn't—" she began, but the words evaporated, caught in the updraft of panic. Amelia lurched toward the podium, tried to get around the first officer, but he blocked her with a gentle sidestep. She gripped the knife fiercely, wheeled and faced the audience, the wig completely crooked, manic eyes flickering over the rows of stunned onlookers.

"I can show you—I can show you the original! They don't want you to know, but—"

Another pair of hands, female this time, landed on Amelia's shoulders, steering her back, but she twisted out of the grip and managed a final lunge at Lily. The second officer caught her at the waist and, with a smooth motion, confiscated the knife and pinned her arms at her sides.

I had seen enough. I crossed the stage in three strides, skidding to a stop between the women. "Let her finish," I said, speaking to Ricci's people as much as to Lily. "Let her speak." Sometimes, the quickest way to defuse lightning is to let the charge find the ground.

With his hands restraining Amelia's arms, the officer turned her toward the audience. "Please, then. Speak."

Amelia, panting, delivered her lines straight into the microphone: "You can't silence me! You can't silence the truth! Lily Davenport built her career on my work—my suffering—my every goddamn page!" But the fire was already waning, the words losing steam in the way most rants will eventually do. On that note, the officers snapped cuffs on her wrists.

"NO! I spent my mum's inheritance and all my life savings to come on this book tour! To get what's due to me. You can't—" Amelia bucked, tried to twist away, but their grip was professional, unyielding. "You're all cowards!" she rasped. "You're letting her get away with it! It's theft—murder—intellectual murder!"

I put a hand on Lily's forearm, a small anchor in the maelstrom. She did not recoil, but I felt a tremor running from her elbow to her shoulder. "You're okay," I said, loud enough that only she would hear.

Ricci's team hustled Amelia off the stage, her feet scuffing across the laminate as she hurled her last, increasingly incoherent insults at the ceiling. "You can't erase me!" came the voice that was losing the battle to distance and the echo of the hallway.

Chapter 36

As the doors closed behind her, I looked out over the crowd—hundreds of faces, all shocked by the possibility that what they'd witnessed might actually be the truth. Or worse, that it was a sideshow, and the real story was waiting for them on the evening news.

In the sudden silence, Lily let go of the podium and almost sat on the floor. I caught her by the elbow, guided her to the chair at the side of the stage. Her legs folded beneath her, and she seemed as stunned as a bombing victim.

I stood between her and the crowd, watching as Ricci herself emerged from the side door, brow furrowed but composed. She gave me a nod; the episode was contained for now.

The moment the doors closed on Amelia and her

convoy of law, the stunned silence ended in a million whispered theories and sidelong glances between strangers who had not expected to witness history, or scandal, or whatever this was supposed to be.

Louisa, bless her, stepped up to the stage, commanding attention in the way only a seventy-something petite British woman could. She adjusted the microphone downward to her height, and the room instantly grew silent.

When all eyes were upon her, my aunt spoke. "This sad and unfortunate event will, no doubt, play out in the courts. However, I would like to say that I, too, was once a writing student of Lily Davenport's, in the same workshop as the woman who disrupted today's reading. I have studied and read the works of both writers, and I will tell you, with all confidence, that the accusations have no basis in fact. I'm sad for this woman who wanted so badly to become successful, but who did not put forth the diligent work it requires to achieve acclaim in a highly competitive field. For those of us in attendance today, we know the answer. We are here because we love Lily Davenport, because she has enriched our lives with her stories. I know Lily would never, ever steal anyone else's work, and I will stand behind her."

The house lights came up. Someone in the audience began to clap—one of those nervous, social-engineered reactions to fill the void. A few others joined in, and by the time I'd helped Lily to her feet, the applause had become a wall of sound. Louisa looked as if she might want to say something else, but realized she should quietly take the win.

Lily stepped forward. I don't know how, but she smiled at her audience and raised one hand to silence them. "Wow. Thank you. If you will give me a moment, I will return and sign books for anyone who would like one."

She turned to me and I walked her off the stage, dimly aware that the event organizer was explaining to the crowd how each row would be called to approach the signing table once the author was ready.

We made our way to the tiny green room where Lily, robbed of all color and possibly ten years of her life, slumped into a chair with a crash. Her breath came in tiny, shallow bursts—somewhere between hyperventilation and hypoxia. Louisa was at her side in seconds, kneeling with both hands wrapped around one of Lily's, as if she could physically draw the trauma from her body.

"It's all right, darling, it's all right," Louisa whispered, and the rhythm of her voice was so steady, so utterly itself, that for a second, I thought Lily might actually believe her.

"You were amazing out there," I added, giving her a bottle of water. "I can't imagine anyone who might have handled it better. Are you sure you're up for signing books?"

She nodded. "I need to. Being among friends and supporters will get me through this."

I hovered at the side, giving Lily a moment to check her makeup and collect herself. Ricci came through the service corridor, looking more like a school principal after a lunchroom riot than a police inspector. She made a beeline for me, her phone pressed to one ear and her eyes flicking constantly.

"We have the suspect in holding," Ricci said. "We'll need statements, obviously, but not at this moment. You take care of your client. I'll send someone when, as you say, the dust settles." She paused. "This is going to be everywhere by morning, yes?"

"Trending already, probably," I said, recalling the

number of phones I'd spotted, and Ricci gave a curt, resigned nod.

On the main stage, the scene was chaos. Amelia's manuscript pages littered the floor, some trampled, some stuck to the laminate. The event staff, busy organizing the attendees into an orderly queue for signed books, were at least keeping people from coming up and helping themselves to the papers. Ricci had started collecting them.

I moved to the podium, knelt, and offered to help gather Amelia's 'exhibits.' The paper was cheap, copier-weight, and the margins were choked with inked lines, arrows, tiny all-caps notes in blue. Each page contained a kind of neurotic cross-referencing that went far beyond her plagiarism accusations. The most damning ones had side-by-side printouts: Amelia's workshop draft, annotated ORIGINAL, next to a passage from Lily's published work, annotated STOLEN. Some had been highlighted in multiple colors, as if the more marker she used, the truer it became.

I scanned a few, searching for actual substance. The sentences were similar, sure, but not identical, and certainly not evidence of theft. If anything, they proved the opposite: the repetitious circuit of someone who had never actually finished a story, only relived it forever.

I turned over the pages to Ricci and returned to the green room. Lily sat staring into the mirror, practicing a smile she surely didn't feel. Louisa rubbed small circles on her back.

The noise from the auditorium swelled, dropped to a hush, then swelled again. Lily met my gaze, took a deep breath, and said, "I need to go back out there." The words were flat, but carried the determination to finish what she'd started, if only to prove she was a professional, still the author of her own life.

Louisa squeezed her hand and nodded. "If you're sure."

I followed as they made their way to the stage steps. The audience, sensing a return to normalcy, fell instantly silent. A few cell phones were out, aimed and ready, but most people watched with something like concern.

Lily paused, took a full breath, and walked to the microphone.

She looked at the remaining debris on the floor, the faces in the crowd, and then—miracle of miracles—she smiled. Not a big smile, not the 'let's pretend this never happened' type, but a thin, exhausted, perfectly human one.

"I'm so sorry you had to witness that," she said, voice pitched slightly above a whisper. "Writing is about sharing, and sometimes it brings out the very best—or the very worst—in us."

A few people laughed nervously, and Lily seized the moment. "If you'd like to ask me about my creative process, or the new book, or really anything else, I promise I'll answer. But if not, I'll understand."

"We love you, Lily!" came a woman's shout from somewhere. A ripple of applause began, cautiously at first, then—when it became clear the ordeal was truly over—open and sustained.

Lily glanced at me, eyes shiny but clear, and I saw that she'd be all right. Shaken, yes, but not broken. She was a survivor, and not only of this day.

She stepped away from the mic, wiped her cheeks with the heel of her hand, and laughed. "At least I guess you could say my events are not boring."

The applause doubled, tripled, and when she turned to leave, the entire room rose in ovation. I watched from the wings as she made her way offstage to the signing table, entering that quiet space where rapport with her fans would rebuild and wounds could start to heal.

* * *

Two hours later, after the slow-motion exodus of the audience with their signed books in hand, and the numbing drop of all adrenaline, Inspector Ricci joined us in the green room with an expression that made me think of someone who had landed a plane on fire. Lily's publisher liaison had stayed by her side from the moment she'd walked off the stage and was here now.

"We require statements," Ricci said, her English clipped and formal, "from all three of you. It is procedure, but also necessary for the prosecutor. Copyright law is outside my experience, so I am not certain how this goes. There may be a complaint, a civil suit, even, but for now—" She glanced at Lily, who looked exhausted—"it is finished."

"Is Amelia all right?" Lily asked. "I mean, she wasn't harmed, was she?"

"Physically, she's fine," I responded. "I'll fill you in later." I could tell Ricci was eager to wind up this whole ordeal so I deferred to her.

She ushered us to a small table and handed out witness forms and pens. The questions were routine: had you ever met the woman before today, did you feel threatened, do you require medical attention? Louisa wrote her responses confidently.

Lily's hand shook so badly she could barely hold the pen, so her publisher's rep took her through the questions, one at a time, reading them aloud and recording her answers, except in cases where she advised Lily not to answer. Apparently, their legal department would step in if or when it went to court.

When we finished, Ricci tucked the forms away and said, "I will call you if there is any further need. You are free to return home, but should be prepared in case this goes into our court system."

Louisa, ever the supporter, wrapped both arms around Lily's shoulders and whispered, "We shall go to the hotel, darling. There's nothing left for us here." She shot a look at me, half command, half plea, and directed one toward the publisher's rep as well. I nodded.

Lily found her voice only as we exited through the service door, where our arranged ride was waiting. The courtyard at the back of the building was silent, washed in late afternoon light and the faint, heavy scent of hot pavement. "Is it really over?" she asked.

"Ricci told me Amelia will be held for psychiatric evaluation, and with luck, she'll get the help she needs. You're safe," I said, with all the calm I could muster.

She nodded, but I could see it wasn't quite real yet.

Louisa herded us down the steps and into the waiting car, where she kept up a stream of bright, empty conversation about the merits of post-event gelato and the superiority of the Roman taxi over all others.

But I watched the rearview, and with every passing kilometer, I wondered if the case was really closed—or if, like all the best stories, this was the cliffhanger and another chapter waited to be written. Lily could have a long ordeal ahead yet; one never knew what a court might do, especially one in a foreign country.

At the traffic circle nearest the library, we passed the holding facility where Amelia would spend the night. The windows were small, but in one of them I caught a flash of movement—a pale oval, followed by a dark shadow. I thought I heard the echo of her voice, though it surely was a trick of the wind: "I will not be erased. Not by her. Not by anyone."

I shook the image out of my head and watched the city slide by, the sun lowering, the future uncertain but at least—if only for tonight—ours.

Chapter 37

The café was called D'Oro, though the only gold inside was the vivid edge of late-afternoon sunlight glazing the marble tabletops. We claimed a corner table. Lily took the seat facing the street, Louisa stationed herself where she could keep an eye on the pastry counter and the restrooms, and I sat with my back to the far wall, the city's flow perfectly framed by centuries-old glass.

We'd stopped at our hotel after the drama of the library event, but none of us wanted to simply hang around and relive it. We were exhausted, but wired, if that made any sense at all. So, we'd set out to see more of this amazing city and find a little something to eat.

Outside, Rome knew nothing of what had happened. Vespas continued to scream down the Corso, tourists choked the crosswalks, and news vans staked out positions in front of a historic building where apparently a political event was taking place, all quietly ignoring us. Inside, the air was thick with the perfume of ground espresso, warm sugar, and the fragrant, resinous trace of old wood polish. Every conversation in the room seemed pitched high enough to drown out our own. Italian outgoingness was perfectly designed for our privacy.

Louisa ordered for all of us. She didn't ask; she simply waved the waiter over and ticked off the items in impeccable Italian: *tre caffè, due tramezzini, una torta di limone.* The man nodded, wrote nothing down, and returned three minutes later with everything, including—because this was Rome—a small bowl of chocolate-dipped biscotti *"per la signora."* I watched Lily's hands as she took her first sip, steady at last.

We ate in silence at first. Louisa devoured two of the sandwich triangles with the rapture of being reunited with an old favorite, and every so often she'd sigh, glance at the window. At one point, she looked at me as if to ask, Did we really live through that?

I had no answer, so I focused on my own espresso, letting the bitterness meld with the tang of the dessert. We must have built up an appetite. The sandwiches were quickly gone, and we ordered more.

Halfway through the second round, Lily set down her cup and reached into her handbag. When her hand reappeared, she slid a crisp white envelope across the table. Her manicure was perfect, but her thumbnail bore a sliver of torn cuticle—a detail I hadn't noticed before.

"For services rendered," she said. Her voice was steadier than it had been in hours, but the words were padded with the formality people use when they're feeling slightly awkward. "And for not bailing out when the going got tough. You truly went above and beyond, Charlie."

I looked at the envelope. It was slender, with my name written on the front—no titles, no flourish. I didn't touch it.

"This isn't necessary."

Lily laughed. "Don't be so American about it. This is business. You—" She stopped, blinked twice, and looked me in the eye. "You saved my life *and* my literary reputation."

I thought about correcting her, about pointing out that all I'd done was show up and keep the odds from getting any worse. But the look on her face—raw with emotion—made me pause. I realized at that moment how much she had feared that loss. Her reputation, clearly, was as dear to her as life itself.

I reached out, pushed the envelope across the table, and kept my hand there until she covered it with her own.

"You survived," I said, not letting her look away. "*You* did that. And if you really want to thank me, go back to London, keep writing your books, and don't let Amelia Morris take another page of your life."

She held the gaze for a long, uncomfortable second and pushed the envelope to my side of the table. She nodded once.

Louisa had been watching the exchange with an indulgent smile for both of us. She finally set down her coffee spoon, clasped her hands in front of her, and announced with impeccable timing, "Well, that settles it. I think I'm retiring as your PI assistant, Charlie. I prefer my ghost tours with actual ghosts and fewer crazies."

She arched an eyebrow at Lily, who managed a real laugh this time—a short, sharp bark that startled the neighboring table.

"Sorry, I shouldn't have branded Amelia in that way. I do realize that she's a tragic figure whose pursuit of credit has destroyed her ability to deserve it. It's sad that her obsession with recognition prevented her from seeing beyond the fact that she needed to keep working and honing her skills, not trying to blame someone else for her lack of success."

We all nodded in agreement. The whole thing had been such a sad situation.

Lily turned to her former student. "You make a formidable bodyguard, Louisa. You and Charlie both."

Louisa preened, brushing invisible crumbs from her lap. "Well then. Perhaps I'll sign on for a future case, so long as it involves fewer stalkers and more *aperitivo*."

In the space of three breaths, the weight that had pressed down on all of us—Lily's terror, my grim responsibility, Louisa's quick improvisation—began to dissolve, tentatively at first and then all at once. It was the laughter of the reprieved, the kind you get only after the worst has happened and you're still upright. I sipped my espresso, savoring the unique flavor, and let the laughter do its work.

The envelope sat there, untouched, its white surface glowing in the late sun. I knew I wouldn't cash the check, but I also knew I'd keep it—perhaps framed for my wall, or filed away with the case notes, a proof that we'd all made it through.

Outside, the city continued. Another day, another thousand stories.

We lingered at the table for another hour. Lily called her publisher, confirming her flight home; Louisa mapped out the next six meals she wanted before leaving Rome; I listened, mostly, content to let the world carry on without me for a while. Every so often, I caught Lily looking at me, a question in her eyes that didn't quite make it to her lips. Perhaps she was thinking of writing this entire adventure into a future book?

When we finally stood to leave, I held the door for both of them. The city was cooling, the light gone soft and blue, and my mind felt at ease.

Some stories end with fireworks. Ours ended with espresso. We would all remember what happened, but we would move on with our lives.

Outside, the news vans were gone.

I watched the sky fade into the Roman dusk, before I followed Louisa and Lily down the street, survivors walking the city that had seen far more drama than we three would ever deliver.

Chapter 38

People forget how the high desert smells and feels on a late summer night. The distinctive tang of ozone from a distant lightning strike, the soft, sneaky sweetness of Russian olive trees, and damp earth after a rain. Sydney had been a bustling wintery respite from summer's heat, Rome a living museum. At home, everything was dry, open, and fresh. I paused before getting into my Jeep at the airport, breathed deeply, and watched the blinking lights of the communication towers atop the Sandias. They were right where I left them. Nice.

Fifteen minutes later, I pulled into my driveway and cut the headlights, sitting in the hush for a minute, listening to the clicking of the engine as it cooled, and savoring the deep, black sky filled with stars. The house—a 1940s ranch style with red-tiled roof—looked half asleep. The porch light haloed the front steps, Drake's little welcome-home message for me. I hefted my computer bag and lifted the handle of my suitcase, so glad this was the last time I would lug this load around, at least for a while.

Inside, the air was cooler, faintly scented with the familiar mix of home and dog. I dropped my bag in the entryway and took two steps before the first missile hit me. Freckles launched herself from the couch and rebounded off my thigh with enough force to get my attention. She barked three times and commenced a full-body wiggle.

Drake stepped out of the bedroom, wearing lightweight pajama pants and not much else. He pulled me into a hug and then a lingering kiss. We both bent down to include Freckles in the pack-hug, a ritual of ours I had sorely missed.

He asked about the trip, but since I'd been texting from airports nonstop for two days, there wasn't much news to share as he carried my bags to the bedroom and set them aside.

"Want a cup of tea or something?" he asked.

"Something." I was already shedding my shoes and unbuttoning my jeans.

"So, you must be sleepy?" Which was code for let's go to bed. We did, and we made up for lost time in the most enjoyable way.

* * *

Due, I suppose, to the transoceanic time warp, I was awake by four. I snuggled in close to my hubby for awhile, but barely dozed, so we got up at six, and I was out with Freckles in the backyard ten minutes later. She made her rounds of the property while I brewed my morning coffee. I lingered by the hedge, mug in hand, and let the high desert light scrub the last traces of European jet lag out of my skull.

Drake, wearing his flight suit and clearly ready to head to the airport to begin a busy day, greeted us with a half-smile and a lovely kiss. He was soon out the door with a mug of coffee and a slice of toast. Life was back to normal.

I needed to go into the office today, get caught up with Ron on what business RJP was dealing with, but first I wanted to unpack and make some sense of all the stuff I'd brought home. This time, it included my well-used Opal train card, a hotel pen I'd carried away from Rome, and three pages of my own case notes, written in a handwriting that had gotten progressively less legible as the week wore on.

Lily had slipped a postcard into my purse at the airport. The front showed a photo of the Pantheon's oculus. On the back, in blue fountain pen: "Thank you for keeping me sane. Someday, we'll laugh about all of it." Signed with a flourish and a lipstick print.

I lined it all up, read my notes one last time, knowing I might be called upon to send them to some law firm, either in London or New York. Rome had been a shitshow, but everyone survived, including Amelia, who'd become the subject of a sympathetic *Daily Mirror* feature and an active GoFundMe for "victims of literary theft." I tamped down a flash of anger at that, knowing the facts as I did. I couldn't decide if the internet made the world more or less just. It definitely kept things interesting.

That was when my phone buzzed.

The email subject line read: "Best Bucket List Adventure Ever!" Only from Louisa.

I clicked open and found myself drawn in.

Dear Charlie—

Have returned to dear, damp England, where the weather is as I left it: sullen and prone to self-pity. My neighbor has new cats (she did not warn me!) and one of them is, I am not kidding, named Percy Bysshe. He is currently trying to seduce me away from the laptop, but I will resist.

I wanted to say, in case I was not clear during that final blur of days in Rome ... You are the best damn partner in crime (and anti-crime) that a woman could hope for. If you ever want to do another case together, please let it be somewhere warm, with better espresso, and fewer deranged Englishwomen in disguise. (Sydney was lovely, but I never really adjusted to the time zone or the concept of "flat white.")

Lily sends her love. She has started writing again. She swears the next one will be dedicated to "the two women who saved my life and my literary dignity." I have doubts about whether we actually did all that, but ... you know.

Will you come to the UK next spring? I have a standing offer from one of my ghost-tour clients to do "afternoon tea with murder" at the Angel Hotel. I can promise you there will be no actual murder, but possibly some very interesting scones.

Text me! Or email. Or send a raven.

Miss you already,

—L.

PS: We understand that Amelia has been returned to England for psychiatric eval (the Italians apparently found her to be a bit much). Lily's attorney believes A will not attempt to press a copyright infringement case. Good news there!

That last bit truly was good news, although not

surprising. On my way home, one of the things I'd used the in-flight wi-fi for was to research the law in regard to intellectual property. I'd learned that story ideas or titles cannot be registered under copyright. Settings and characters were generally too vague to count. The law protects against plagiarism, the exact copying of someone else's work, and we'd clearly seen that did not apply to Amelia's allegations against Lily.

I re-read the email, and on the second go, I caught the line about "best partner in crime," and felt my face warm with the affection I'd long held for Louisa. I tried to imagine my life without her: less complicated, sure, but also infinitely more boring.

I replied:
Dear L,

Sydney is a distant hallucination, Rome even more so, but the dog refuses to let me sleep in. That should improve once I adapt to our mile-high elevation here.

I accept your invitation to London, provided we can do at least one afternoon tea where no one is arrested. Please tell Lily I'm solidly in her corner.

As for being partners, I can't imagine doing it any other way. Next time, you pick the country, and I'll pack extra Post-its.

Glad we're all alive, and that we all get to tell the story.
—C

I hit send, leaned back and stared at the screen, wondering what *normal* would feel like after all this. Before I formed an answer, my phone buzzed, this time with a photo: Louisa, in her scarf and quirky smile, hoisting a huge mug of tea. I laughed, and the sound startled Freckles, who came running in to check on me.

I scratched her ears, reached beside my chair for an old tennis ball, and tossed it across the room. The sound of claws on hardwood echoed through the house. In the silence that followed, I felt the residue of recent weeks finally drain away.

I sipped my coffee, watched the sunlight peek over the Sandias, casting its light over the city, and I smiled. Normal.

Another adventure would come along. It always did. And when it did, I'd be ready.

Author Notes

More than twenty years ago, I was teaching writing courses, plugging along with my own novels, and generally doing whatever it took to survive as an author (the first bestseller list appearance was *years* away). Once I quit the teaching gig, I remained in contact with several former students and followed their careers as some of them went on to publication. At one point when we were talking about one of the elderly ladies who'd taken the class and stayed in touch with me, my dear hubby remarked something like, "Do you ever worry that one of those ladies will latch on and start following you a little *too* closely?"

I still have no idea what he meant by that—it never happened. But the question did stick in my mind as a what-if for a future story idea. Sometimes it takes the tiniest fragment of an idea with me, and a fictional plot is off and running.

This story was a long time in the making, and it needed the perfect backdrop. For that, I want to thank my lovely daughter and granddaughter for providing the oomph I needed to get myself halfway around the world to Sydney. Ashley, you were the perfect tour guide in your home city. Stephanie, you looked out for all those pesky travel details I didn't care to mess with. It was the perfect mother-daughter-granddaughter reunion-slash-work trip and it was wonderful being pampered by the two of you.

I will admit that I took artistic license with the placement of bookshops and restaurants. None of those are meant to mimic real ones. However, certain of the incidents described here actually did happen to us (a lorikeet stealing sugar packets from a table at a sidewalk restaurant), and some real places captured the imagination (the so-called 'secret garden' where the pathway led downward from the street to an amazingly bucolic experience in the very middle of a major city). Those are the types of experiences you cannot find on a tour itinerary, the ones that I will never forget.

The most emotional scene in the book, for me, came near the end when Lily's audience supports her after the crazy amount of drama. Because, dear readers, it truly is all about you. We write stories so readers can enjoy them, and it means the world to receive the positive feedback from those with whom a book has resonated. Thank you, from my very core.

No book of mine would be complete without my added thanks to my editing and beta reading team. From extra spaces between words to great catches in spelling proper names, I'm always amazed at the number of things I miss, which you catch. Stephanie Dewey, Sandra Anderson, Susan Gross, Marcia Koopmann, Isobel Tamney, and Paula Webb—I'm proud to have you on my team. You are the best!

Thank you for taking the time to read *Bestsellers Can Be Murder*. If you enjoyed it, please consider telling your friends or posting a short review. Word of mouth is an author's best friend and is much appreciated.

Thank you,
Connie

* * *

**Sign up for Connie Shelton's free mystery newsletter at connieshelton.com
and receive advance information about new books, along with a chance at prizes, discounts and other mystery news!**

**Contact by email: connie@connieshelton.com
Follow Connie Shelton on Pinterest, Facebook, Instagram, and Twitter (X)**

Scan the QR code to discover more!

Books by Connie Shelton

The Charlie Parker Series
Deadly Gamble
Vacations Can Be Murder
Partnerships Can Be Murder
Small Towns Can Be Murder
Memories Can Be Murder
Honeymoons Can Be Murder
Reunions Can Be Murder
Competition Can Be Murder
Balloons Can Be Murder
Obsessions Can Be Murder
Gossip Can Be Murder
Stardom Can Be Murder
Phantoms Can Be Murder
Buried Secrets Can Be Murder
Legends Can Be Murder
Weddings Can Be Murder
Alibis Can Be Murder
Escapes Can Be Murder
Old Bones Can Be Murder
Sweethearts Can Be Murder
Money Can Be Murder
Road Trips Can Be Murder
Cruises Can Be Murder
Deceptions Can Be Murder
Bestsellers Can Be Murder
Holidays Can Be Murder - a Christmas novella

The Ben Pecos Mystery Series
(continued from author Susan Slater)
The Homecoming

The Samantha Sweet Cozy Mystery Series

Sweet Masterpiece
Sweet's Sweets
Sweet Holidays
Sweet Hearts
Bitter Sweet
Sweets Galore
Sweets Begorra
Sweet Payback
Sweet Somethings
Sweets Forgotten
Spooky Sweet
Sticky Sweet
Sweet Magic
Deadly Sweet Dreams
The Ghost of Christmas Sweet
Tricky Sweet
Haunted Sweets
Secret Sweets
Garden Sweets
Spellbound Sweets – a Halloween novella
Thankful Sweets – a Thanksgiving novella
The Woodcarver's Secret – the series prequel

The Heist Ladies Series

Diamonds Aren't Forever
The Trophy Wife Exchange
Movie Mogul Mama
Homeless in Heaven
Show Me the Money

www.ingramcontent.com/pod-product-compliance
Lightning Source LLC
LaVergne TN
LVHW091536060526
838200LV00036B/626